THE DUST DESTROYER

In cars, trains, buses and tube, the one topic of conversation was the black sky and mysterious disappearance of dust. It was remarkable, too, how incredibly well washed and neat everybody looked, from the grimiest labourer to the proprietress of a beauty salon. Dust was on the march, from skins, clothes, streets, buildings—everywhere. Even the slums, rotten with the accumulated dirt of years, were bright and resplendent, something for the train travelers to gaze upon in stunned wonder.

This removal of dust seemed to be a boon to mankind—but it turned out to be a deadly scourge, and unless it was stopped millions of people would die!

THE GOLDEN AMAZON SAGA

THE DUST DESTROYER

JOHN RUSSELL FEARN

Edited by Philip Harbottle

WILDSIDE PRESS

THE DUST DESTROYER

CONTENTS

THE DUST DESTROYER

CHAPTER 1

The Great Idea

Timothy Brown ran the tip of his index finger along the polished top of the mahogany sideboard and frowned to himself. His action had left enough imprint behind for him to write his name, had he chosen. Not that anybody would have cared particularly anyhow since Timothy Brown was only a solicitor's clerk with vague leanings towards physics in his spare time. In a word, he was not important.

"Fairly crawling with dust," he muttered. "Can't imagine what the woman does with her time!"

He looked at the sideboard again, and then around the room itself. It was pretty much the same as any well-used living room—untidy, filled with furniture more accommodating than beautiful, and definitely everything was dusty.

"Dust!" Timothy murmured again; then he listened for a moment to the sizzling of frying emanating from the adjoining room of the little flat—the room called 'kitchenette' by the landlord and several other things by those who used it.

"Elsie!!" Timothy Brown bawled suddenly.

"What d'you want? Can't you hear I'm busy?"

Timothy Brown scratched the end of his long, somewhat purplish nose. He found it devilishly difficult to be the master in his own abode sometimes. But this dust! He just had to put his foot down.

"Can't help it if you are busy!" he shouted. "Come here."

Elsie came—slowly. She was a short, over-broad woman with a pendulous bust. Her flabby forearms were bare and shiny with cooking grease. Her face had once been pretty but had degenerated into a shapeless grey in which her features had a curious flowed-together quality. She was nearly fifty—and looked it.

"Do you want your tea or don't you?" she asked bluntly. "Fish won't cook itself, remember."

"I'm not interested in the fish at the moment, Elsie. What about this dust?"

"Well, what about it?" Elsie challenged.

"Are you my wife, or are you not? Do you run this place in my absence, or do you just sit around in the muck and read these damned things?"

Elsie watched in smouldering calm as her husband whipped up a fistful of her favourite women's weeklies and brandished them.

"I'll read what I like when I like," she said. "And you can't stop me! Place is clean enough—"

"It isn't," Timothy retorted. "It takes up that much confounded room in the place I can't turn round for it!"

"As for the dust, I clean up every day. I can't help it settling, can I?" Elsie said. "Look here…!"

Suddenly purposeful she strode to the window and whipped back the curtains. The gloomy November night had closed down at four-thirty and by now—six-fifteen—was absolute. The glow of light from the window fanned out onto a deepening fog drifting up the narrow street outside.

"What's that got to do with your cleaning up?" Timothy asked acidly.

"Everything! If you want to be free of dust, or almost, then get yourself into a job where we can go and live on the sea coast instead of this rotten hole in the depths of east London!"

Probably Elsie would have said a good deal more but for the fact that a blue haze from the kitchenette and violent sizzlings impelled her on her way. Timothy hardly noticed her go: he was gazing out into the fog, a man lost in bottomless speculations. Small, nondescript and dyspeptic though he was he had a mind capable of conceiving the most incredible things—and more often than not these things were scientific.

"Fog…dust," he mused. "Distinct relationship. Stop the dust and you stop the fog."

His speculations did not end here even though his next action was entirely habitual. He moved to the table, propped the evening paper against the milk jug—and then waited for Elsie to serve the meal.

Presently she did so, and not with any good grace, either. Absently he took the filled teacup she handed him and then ate the indifferently cooked fish whilst he skimmed through the evening's news.

"Four ships have been lost at sea in the worst fog for years," he said presently. "Even radar didn't help them. Maybe this is something of the same thing drifting in here. Did you get the weather forecast?"

Elsie's response sounded something like "Umph!" and Timothy glanced up in irritation. He discovered she was buried in one of her women's papers, the cover of which revealed a too-good-to-be-true hero drooping over an incredibly curvaceous heroine.

"Did you get the weather forecast?" Timothy demanded, banging the table.

"Why should I?"

"I want to know if the fog is likely to continue."

Even Elsie was stirred at this and she looked up in amazement.

"What on earth does it matter? You'll have to go to work, fog or no fog, won't you?"

"It's nothing to do with my going to work. I might try an experiment with the fog if it lasts for a day or two."

Elsie put down her knife and fork. "Oh no, you don't! No more experiments! I haven't forgotten the last one when you nearly blew us out of house and home!"

Timothy cleared his throat. "Fog," he found himself saying out loud, "Is caused by dust particles, Elsie, therefore fog and dust are very closely allied."

"Oh, so you're on that dust business again, are you?"

Timothy avoided his wife's malignant glare. "The particles are about nought point nought nought one of an inch in diameter. They may be composed of evaporated ocean spray, disintegrated dust from shooting stars or meteorites, volcanic discharge—almost anything. And fog particles are bound to have some kind of dust for their nucleus."

"Humph," Elsie agreed, chewing steadily as she read her periodical.

"I've visited quite a few small scientific laboratories and in one of them I saw quite an ingenious instrument. It contained a pump, a lens, filter papers, and a glass plate divided into millimetres. Samples of air can be sucked into this apparatus and the number of dust particles determined. Do you realize," Timothy went on, raising his fish-server dramatically, "that in a crowded city like this there are about one hundred thousand dust particles to the cubic centimetre? Over the ocean the amount is lowered to only two thousand per cubic centimetre."

"Which bears out what I said," Elsie put in. "Live on the coast and then you'll be happy. Or, at any rate, I will."

"I am trying," Timothy said, with monstrous calm, "to state a scientific theory. Even if you do not understand at least do me the favour of listening."

Elsie made a grimace and set aside her paper. She ate, and waited, her blue eyes unintentionally very vacant.

"Take twilight," Timothy said presently, with a flourish.

"Why?"

"Because it suits my purpose! Twilight only happens because of the refraction of dust particles—the dusty, translucent curtain through which the sun's rays have to pass."

"I don't remember you bothering about that m the old days when we used to stroll down Norton's lane of an evening."

Timothy sighed. "We were different then, Elsie. Young and inexperienced, otherwise we— But I'm straying from the subject. Raindrops and hailstones all have a particle of dust within them which serves as the original point upon which to condense. Again, when condensation is sufficiently vigorous the water vapour becomes small globules of water with dust specks as their centre—hence clouds!"

Elsie yawned a little behind her hand and resumed eating. As far as Timothy was concerned his fish might have been on another world for all the attention he paid to it. There was a glimmer in his pale grey eyes, which meant he was getting warmed up to his subject.

"Take volcanic dust! The eruption of the Krakatoa volcano in Java in August 1883 sent dust twenty miles into the air. That dust impregnated the whole atmospheric envelope and took years to descend. That occurrence provided mankind with some of the most glorious sunrises and sunsets in history. Yet dust is also a deadly enemy. Elsie, and the root cause of many a disease. You know how the soap manufacturers make a point of dust when advertising their wares."

"If all this is building up to my cleaning down that sideboard, Timothy, you can think again! I haven't the time; nor am I as nimble as I used to be!"

"You can forget the sideboard," Timothy answered absently. "If the idea I have in mind works out you may never have to dust anything again."

Elsie dropped her fork. "What! Now look here, just what do you mean by that? If you're planning something to get rid of me I'll—"

"Oh, don't be so ridiculous! What I mean is that I have a theory at the back of my mind, which may eliminate dust—not only for you but for everybody else. One of the biggest curses of mankind's daily life completely removed! That certainly would be something."

"In fact, another scientific experiment?"

There was a quiet firmness about Timothy's voice, which Elsie knew only too well. Nothing would prevent him tinkering with his idea, even if he blew the whole building to pieces before he had finished. So she did not argue: she just let him be and returned to reading her periodical.

She was still reading an hour later when it dawned on her that Timothy had disappeared from the tea table. She looked about her, failed to see him, and shrugged to herself. Laboriously she got to her feet and began the onerous task of clearing the tea things. Timothy, she noticed, had not finished his fish and there still remained half a cup of cold tea.

When he did not return towards ten o'clock she began to feel uneasy. Just about like him to have gone out into the fog and lost himself! But, when she checked up on the hat stand she found his outdoor clothes hanging there as usual. He was still in the flat somewhere.

He was—comfortably in bed, surrounded by bulky volumes. When Elsie finally tracked him down she discovered him immersed in Soddy's *Matter and Energy*, and pungent smoke pouring from a battered briar.

"So here you are! At least you might have told me where you were going!"

"I did. You were so wrapped up in that infernal love story you didn't even hear—"

"And stop smoking! You know I don't like it in the bedroom!"

"You'll have to tolerate it for this once, m'dear. I can't think without my pipe and I've got to think tonight as I have never thought before!"

It was not only for that night, either, but for many weeks that Timothy Brown went about with an air of deep preoccupation. He found the normal run of life, particularly at the office, exceedingly irksome. When he wished to give his mental attention to atoms and energies he found himself busy with conveyances, affadavits, and other pedantry of the law. At home he was nearly mute, disregarding Elsie's grumbles.

Almost every evening he brought some electrical gadget or other and finally, about a month after he had been hit with his original idea, he set about the job of assembling all the stuff he had collected, working from a diagram drawn in an exercise book.

Timothy was tampering with the basic forces of Nature without being scientist enough to know what he really was doing.

His main idea was to lift from the world the curse of dust to make lighter the drudgery of the housewife. Certainly he had a brilliant idea in mind but, unfortunately, he had not the insight to foresee the possible repercussions. One cannot alter a vital constituent of Nature without producing a terrific reaction somewhere.

Elsie, never possessing any claims to genius, and even less to scientific insight, could only dumbly watch the growth of a mysterious instrument, its insides filled with all manner of vari-coloured wires and identification tags. Her husband, after many nights of mysterious testing of this apparatus—which he kept locked away in a steel deed cabinet in the wardrobe while he was at the office—never attempted to explain what he was up to. That came a week before Christmas when he arrived home looking mysteriously pleased with himself.

Elsie gave him a morose look. As usual she was untidy and grease-smudged, but at least she had prepared a tea well worth having. When it came to cooking she was in her right sphere—and Timothy knew it.

"I have a surprise for you, m'dear," he said, when the meal was over.

"Are there any more?" Elsie asked, in a stunned kind of voice.

"More? Oh, I see what you mean! My experiments of the last few weeks. Well, my surprise is connected with those. I want you to dress in your very best, and quickly, in readiness to meet Mr. Jacob Foster."

"Who's Jacob Foster?" Elsie could be so infuriatingly dull sometimes.

"He's the managing director of the Kleen Sweep Brush Company. A very big man and a very big company. You've surely heard of him?"

"No. And I can't think why he should come here."

"He's coming to see my dust-destroyer. If he's satisfied, I shall be worth a fortune. Briefly Elsie, I am going into the dust-removing business. Or rather the Kleen Sweep Company is. All we have to do is sit and collect. I am so confident of success I quit my job today."

Elsie jumped, really stung this time. "You what!"

Timothy only smiled. "Nothing to fear, m'dear. I have the idea of the century. You'll know all about it when Mr. Foster gets here. Now do get yourself cleaned up."

Elsie muttered something not entirely complimentary, and shuffled from the room. Forty-five minutes later she returned and even Timothy had to admit she did not look half bad. He could even see why he had once admired her. Pity time had been so unkind to her face and figure.

"What about you?" she asked, adjusting her earrings and looking meanwhile at the gadget on the cleared table.

Timothy did not answer this for the flat bell had just rung long and resolutely. He adjusted his tie, smoothed his jacket, then headed from the room. Elsie gave an anxious glance around the perpetual untidiness and stood on one foot then on the other—until presently after murmuring in the minute hallway Jacob Foster was ushered in.

Elsie blinked and waited, then the moment she was introduced she found her hand seized in a steel grasp and her arm was pumped relentlessly.

"Ah, Mrs. Brown, a delight indeed! You are fortunate indeed to have so ingenious a husband."

"Am I? Oh, yes— Er, I suppose so."

Elsie stopped talking, aware that Jacob Foster was about six-feet-four in height, enormous in circumference, and very red-faced. He possessed a tremendous mane of black hair, which bobbed in the oddest fashion every time he moved his head.

"Cold even for this time of year," he commented genially, unbolting the belt of his stupendous overcoat.

"Very," Elsie said meekly, watching Timothy fussing around the Gadget.

"Christmas will soon—" the great man began, but Timothy dared to cut him short.

"There it is, sir," he said breathlessly. "My apologies for asking you to come to see the apparatus here, but I want to be absolutely sure nothing goes wrong at the initial experiment. You do understand?"

"Definitely!" Foster seated himself upon a chair, which creaked ominously and waved a fat red hand. "I am at your service, sir. What exactly do you propose to do?"

"I propose," Timothy said, in a firm, clear voice, "to completely destroy dust. I mentioned that when I called upon you."

"Quite, quite. But destroying dust is not new. My own world famous Kleen Sweep Silent Vacuums destroy every trace of dust wherever it is used. According to our latest statistical report there were two million users of—"

"Yes, Mr. Foster, but you do not really destroy dust. You just remove it."

"Is this a time to split hairs?" the big man asked, and his red face opened in a gigantic grin.

"I think it is. I—totally—destroy—dust!"

Famous statements by equally famous statesmen had never possessed such portent as those four deliberate words of Timothy Brown's, though he and the world were not aware of it—then. They produced a kind of sobering silence, in which Elsie hardly dared to breathe.

"First, to demonstrate," Timothy said, and without difficulty he picked up his Gadget and slung it to his shoulder by a canvas strap specially devised for the purpose. Then he moved across the room to the sideboard and ran his finger along the polished top. His expression changed and he looked at Elsie.

"Yes, I dusted it," she said coldly.

"But why?" Timothy nearly yelled. "I wanted it for a demonstration— Oh, never mind!" He stormed impatiently across to the bureau and peered carefully along the top of it. Then he smiled and rubbed his hands.

"Satisfactory?" Foster asked, watching in wonder.

"Eminently. A thin film of dust."

"Oh," the big man said, seeming vaguely astonished that a man should take pride in having thick dust on the top of the bureau.

"The actual job is simple," Timothy continued. "Just connect this apparatus to the ordinary power point, and its interior workings do the rest, Now watch closely— You can see all right there. Mr. Foster?"

"Perfectly. The light is oblique."

Timothy nodded and raised the curious camera-like front of his instrument. Then he switched on a button. Beyond a buzzing noise nothing appeared to happen. He kept the machine running for perhaps half a minute and then switched off. When he ran his finger along the bureau top he left no trail, and on the end of his finger was absolute cleanness.

Foster lumbered to his feet and inspected the bureau intently from every angle of light. When at last he looked up sharply his eyes appeared a little bloodshot with excitement.

"That's marvellous, Mr. Brown! Absolutely marvellous! No suction, no draught, and yet you removed the dust!"

"I destroyed it!" Timothy insisted, "I cannot stress that fact too much. This invention, Mr. Foster, makes your most efficient vacuum cleaner a child's toy by comparison. This is a scientifically balanced conception which can, in time, remove all dust from the world—completely."

"I see," Foster said heavily, straightening up. "Could you explain how?"

"Certainly. As the inventor, why not? I can explain without giving myself away—if you know what I mean."

"Quite so." Foster sat down again and Timothy dropped his Gadget on the table. Elsie eased herself with great difficulty into the fireside chair and waited.

"Technically." Timothy said, "this instrument is a dust vibrator. You are aware, I suppose, that a dust particle—like any other particle of matter—is composed of atoms, and that these atoms, when aggregated, comprise a molecule?"

"Of course," Foster agreed, with intense gravity.

"Very well. You will know also that the electron is essential to the structure of an atomic formation, and the atomic formation to the structure of the molecule. Now, it is possible that in time the atoms would lose many of their electrons due to the terrific velocity with which the latter move. The disappearance of all electrons would make the weight of the molecule too heavy for the atom to support, and the result would be collapse."

"Quite," Foster said, and eased his collar.

"That occurrence would take time. I don't wish to say exactly how long for the simple reason that I have evolved a way of destroying all the electrons within the molecules, which go to make up a dust particle. The result is collapse of the molecule, and incidentally collapse of the dust particle."

"Stupendous!" Foster's stare was what is known as 'glassy'.

"The electrons can be disrupted by vibration. Not an actual force, but a shifting plane of disturbances powerful enough to destroy them. The result is a complete absence of dust wherever the vibrations touch. That clear?"

"Eh—yes, within limits." The business side in Foster was rising. He was not a scientist but a man of commerce, and he had to know all about a product before he gave an opinion on it. So he posed a question.

"How do you actually do this trick? You've just skated around the edge, so to speak."

"I know." Timothy answered calmly. "We have no agreement, so of course I—"

"Yes, yes, I appreciate your caution. You'd be a fool if you didn't safeguard yourself. But surely you have this thing patented?"

"Definitely! But even then—" Timothy stopped beating around the bush. "I asked you here tonight for a demonstration, Mr. Foster, and I have given it. Is this machine of interest to you, or not? If it is, let us sign a provisional contract, for you to have complete monopoly of the idea. If you are not interested then we'll shake hands and remain friends."

Foster rose, his great hand extended. "My very dear sir, I am more than satisfied with what I have seen. I just want to know how it works, to be sure that my manufacturing end can secure the necessary materials—"

"There'll be no difficulty, I assure you."

"Very well, then. As it happens "I have a provisional agreement here which—"

"I have a better one," Timothy interrupted, producing it.

"After spending most of my life as a solicitor's clerk I think I can be relied on to handle the legal side. Tell me what you think of this—"

Dense silence descended as the great man brooded over the clauses—and five minutes later the provisional contract had been signed and Foster was back again on his precarious chair.

"I'll make the scientific fundamentals as clear as I can," Timothy said. "An electron is pure negative electricity, and electricity, if one gets down to fundamentals, is vibration in a certain form—a vibration of such a periodicity that it becomes light. My vibration is below that of light. It is invisible but very destructive. It repels and smashes an electron completely. Normal electricity is converted into vibration inside my machine, and the bombardment of dust electrons takes place."

"Yes, but how do you confine yourself just to dust?" Foster asked. "If you destroy dust atoms, or whatever they are, why don't you destroy all other matter as well?"

"Because there are molecules of different orders. True, certain things may break down as well as dust, but it is a million to one against it happening. Just as with an ordinary electrical instrument the user might be killed. It is the unknown factor—just one of those things.

In this machine of mine,"—Timothy tapped it gently— "negative electrical energy is transformed into vibration and hurled at the atomic structure of dust particles, with the result that they collapse. You see the advantage? No dust bag to empty, no awkward corners to get into, just project the lens where the dust is, and switch on."

"This," Foster breathed, surging to his feet again, "Is about the cleverest idea I ever heard of. Might I ask how you happened onto it?"

"Oh, just a chain of reasoning." Timothy shrugged his lean shoulders. "I thought of dust and studied a fog— then I put my scientific kink to work—and the machine finally emerged. I'm sure you'll find a ready sale for it."

"You have complete drawings, of course, and all details?"

"Everything. On the signing of our final agreement tomorrow I'll hand everything over to you."

CHAPTER 2

Nature gone mad

Towards six a.m. the following morning Timothy awoke, and after a brief analysis of his thoughts—a daily practice—decided that he was reasonably contented with life. The contract would be signed today; he would collect a considerable sum in advance royalties; and no longer would he have to drudge in the office. He could pursue science or live in retirement, as the mood suited him. Yes—an excellent prospect.

It was still dark, and bitterly cold. Shivering as he emerged he slipped into dressing gown and slippers and then floundered sleepily from the dark bedroom.

Entering the kitchenette Timothy switched on the light in the usual way, and then blinked a little. It seemed unbearably bright, or else his eyes were still sleep-deadened. He looked about him, remarking the crystal clarity of everything. The light literally blazed back from shining pots and pans, gleaming knives, spotless tilework around the sink. Yes, even the greasy old gas cooker looked like new.

"Elsie has sure put in some work here," Timothy murmured, putting the water on to boil. "Maybe "I shouldn't scold her too much in future. She's done wonders."

Nonetheless he was a bit puzzled. As he remembered it, when he had come in here the previous evening to wash his hands, the place had been as indifferently clean as usual. Yet now there was not a mark anywhere. Even the linolelum was so clean that the pattern stood out brilliantly.

"Pleasant, but peculiar," Timothy told himself, and yawned over the still cold kettle.

With time to kill he wandered into the living room and switched on the lights. Here again the brilliance struck him like a physical blow and made him close his eyes for a moment. Accustoming himself he just stood gazing, wrestling with a deep, unexplained problem. The walls were so clean they might have been redecorated. The usually grimy ceiling was snow white. The curtains were immaculate. The carpet looked as though it had just been laid. As for his precious sideboard, the shine on it was as magnificent as the day when it had left the hands of the original polisher.

Timothy hovered on the edge of possibilities then hurried back into the kitchenette as he heard the water boiling. He made the tea and returned to the bedroom. Elsie grumbled sleepily as he switched on the light over the bed.

"What did you want to change the bulb for?" she complained, when at last she could see properly. "You know I don't like a glare in the bedroom."

"I haven't changed anything—at least as far as bulbs are concerned," Timothy answered absently. "Here's your tea."

"Thanks."

They drank in silence for a while; then Timothy asked a question.

"Tell me something, Elsie. Have you been cleaning things i up downstairs?"

"Are you still grousing at me?" she snapped.

"No. I just want to know." Then, since Elsie's look was sufficient Timothy went on, "That settles it then. It's that dust destroyer of mine. Can't be anything else. The bright lights, the spotless walls, no dirt anywhere. Even the filthiest old parts of the kitchen stove look as though they've come from a showroom!"

"Eh?" Elsie stared at him. "What did you say?"

Timothy repeated everything and added patiently. "Just wait until you look for yourself, then you'll see."

"But—but how could your gadget do that? You only tried it on the bureau. It couldn't clean the house out by itself, could it?"

"Definitely not. But there is one point I may have overlooked, and that is chain reaction."

"What the dickens is that?"

"Reaction from one atomic aggregate to another. You know how sometimes on the stage one chorus girl falls over and the rest just crumple up one after the other? Well, that's chain reaction. Sort of. Could be dangerous," Timothy finished vaguely, which remark deserved to be recorded as the greatest understatement of all time.

"Anyway, it's time you were getting dressed," Elsie decided. "You'll be late for—" She remembered and looked worried. "Tim, you really meant it when you said you'd quit?"

"I did. Don't let it worry you."

"But it does! What happens if the money dries up? We're not all that well off."

"But we will be, never fear. Just the same I had better be getting dressed. I promised Foster to be at his office at ten."

With that Timothy collected the two empty teacups and then hurried out to the bathroom. While he washed and shaved the dawn came, pale against the stained glass window—and because the window was opaque Timothy Brown was again delayed in observing the full effect of his amazing dust destroyer. He completed his ablutions in the midst of a glare of light flashing back from argent tiling, then returned to the bedroom to dress. He found Elsie seated on the edge of the bed, a gross figure in her nightdress, staring through the window.

"For heaven's sake, what's the matter?" Timothy demanded impatiently. "Are you trying to catch your death of cold? And either draw the curtains or switch off the light. Do you want everybody to see you?"

"It's the end of the world," Elsie muttered. "It can't be anything else!"

Timothy frowned and moved to her side, following the direction of her gaze. What he saw nearly paralyzed him with shock. For outside that window was the weirdest dawn ever!

The sun was fairly well clear of the horizon and in its accustomed place, shining over the top of Caldwell's Bakery; but what in the name of Satan had happened to it? It was a blindingly brilliant blue-white ball, its edges festooned with mighty streamers of red, which curled majestically to an unimaginable distance in space. Around him hung a pearly glow, unforgettably beautiful but painful to the eyes.

And if this was not enough, the stars were shining with intense clearness in a dense black sky.

"The end of the world," Elsie repeated. "Tim, I'm scared. Something awful's going to happen! There's never been a sky like that before!"

"Take it easy," Timothy whispered, his face sweating. "There's a scientific explanation if I can just put my finger on it. We're looking at the sun as it appears in outer space, and yet there is air because we're breathing it. Surely it couldn't be the—"

He did not dare say it. In any case words were failing him again because the view outside was so fascinating. The naked, unbelievable sun was shining upon roofs that had become magically new, as though armies of cleaners had spent the night scrubbing the city clean. Usually, from this window, there was a drab vision of infinities of grey slate carved up into uninspiring boxes. Just at this point of the east end private property vied with commercial enterprise—which was one reason why Caldwell's Bakery rose up like a shining monument, its usually filthy chimney now a gleaming red funnel of polished brick.

"Oh, Lor'!" Timothy Brown gasped, and sat down beside his wife with a sudden thud. She gave him a vacant look.

"Maybe it's that chain reaction," Timothy said. "Tell you what, the radio may say something—"

He hurtled out of the room, gown flying behind him, and almost tumbled on top of the radio, switching it on. After a second or two it picked up in mid-sentence.

"…not known yet whether the phenomenon is temporary or permanent. Physical scientists are now at work trying to determine the nature of the mystery, which appears to be a complete inversion of natural law. It is reported that the effect is at the moment confined to the eastern side of London, but that it is rapidly spreading. Elsewhere in the country, conditions are normal. Everybody in the east London radius is urged to exercise caution, particularly out of doors, where shadows are extremely dangerous."

Timothy switched off again in a daze, scarcely remembered dressing. When finally he came to himself he was at the breakfast table with Elsie handing him bacon with one hand and the morning paper with the other.

"Just look at that!" she insisted, planking the paper down. "I tell you it's the end of the world. I always knew Judgment Day might come: it's a contravention of physical laws and I'm filled with the horrible foreboding that I may be the root cause of it."

His eyes dropped to the newspaper and remained on the biggest headlines since the declaration of World War II—

NATURE GONE MAD!

After this there followed long columns written by teams of reporters, some of them claiming to be 'scientific correspondents' and having a field day airing their views. Such things as defraction and refraction were discussed at great length, and some writers even extracted joy from the fact that mankind was being treated to a view of the sky as it must always look from outer space.

"And every one of these reporters is wrong," Timothy said morosely, tackling his bacon. "I'm about the only man in the world who knows what's really happened, with the possible exception of Foster. I don't think he's scientist enough, though, to tumble to the truth. At least I hope not or my deal with him is going to fall through."

"What are you talking about?" Elsie demanded, fear bringing a sharp edge to her voice. "How on earth can you be responsible for this weird sky and sun outside?"

Timothy glanced about him. The electric light was still on, blazing brilliantly. Outside, the city loomed savagely bright where the sunlight touched.

"Notice anything about this room, or any of the rooms where we have had the light on?" Timothy asked. "The shadows have gone. There are not many anyhow with the light right overhead, but what there were have disappeared. And do you know why? Because dust helps to create shadows. When there is none they are greatly lessened. But outside, where the sun shines, the law of diffusion, always caused by dust, has gone."

"I don't know what you're talking about," Elsie said flatly.

"Maybe you will before I've finished. In the ordinary way when you go into a shadow on a sunny street you can still see your way, can't you?"

"Naturally!"

"Well, that is because dust in the air diffuses the sunlight and reflects it into the areas where no actual sunlight is shining. When dust is absent the shadows are like black ink, as though there were no air at all. Just the same as it is on the moon. That's why the radio warning said the shadows are extremely dangerous."

Elsie looked as though she might be taking it in.

"As for the black sky, that's absence of dust again," Timothy went on moodily. "It looks blue and has cloud because of dust. Remove that and the sky turns black. You take away the diffusive screen and: therefore the sun looks as it does from outer space and the stars shine in the day time."

"But how in the world could your gadget cause all this?"

"I keep telling you! Chain reaction! I started the whole thing when I destroyed the molecules of dust on top of the bureau. I thought the whole thing would end there, but evidently it didn't. Once I started the destructive process the thing must have gone on and on, wiping out dust molecules at an incredible rate. During the night the effect must have radiated outwards from this flat to encompass most of east London, travelling upwards into the atmosphere as well! I suppose all neighbours of ours are aware by now that their flats are as spotless as ours and they're probably scratching their heads to determine why!"

Timothy wheeled round in his chair and gazed through the window. The sun was higher now and hidden by the angle of the building, so it was possible to look out upon a city that was weirdly beautiful. Everywhere the sun touched, the bright buildings reflected it scintillatingly; but everywhere there was a shadow there was blackest ink. And to judge from the incessant blaring of horns from the street there was trouble with the traffic, too.

"And spreading!" Elsie said bitterly. "The announcer said so. Only thing you can do is stop it!"

"I can't."

"What do you mean, can't? You must! If you don't you'll be—" Elsie stopped, not quite sure of the issues involved. She only knew that she was so overwhelmingly terrified that she felt sick.

"I daren't tell anybody," Timothy whispered, disinclined to eat. "I might get arrested, or even charged with murder, or something. My God, what a mess!"

"Mess is right! And to get back to cases, what about your job? If Foster gets to know your infernal gadget can cause this sort of thing he's not going to be very anxious to do business, is he? In fact you surely wouldn't let him in for such a—a disaster?"

"No, of course not." Timothy gave her a mournful glance. "On the other hand I don't know if old Meadows would take me back in the office. He might—"

"Better go and find out, otherwise we're going to be in the workhouse."

Timothy nodded, realizing he was rapidly sinking back into the old rut of conveyances, mortgages, and affadavits. He ignored the remainder of his breakfast and made preparations for departure. Then at last, after his farewell of the still tremulous Elsie, he stepped out into the mad world.

Almost instantly he became aware of pale, frightened faces staring up at the black skies. There was another thing he noticed, as he hurried on foot through the streets to his own place of employment, the real danger of the shadows. When he passed out of the sunlight it was like going underground, the vision of sunlit buildings across the street casting no reflected light worth mentioning. Time and again he blundered into men and women and they, like him, muttered uneasy apologies and stumbled on their way.

When he finally arrived at Barton, Barton, and Meadows he was scared and perspiring. So far none of the junior staff had arrived. Even in the ordinary way they were never punctual and today they literally had a heaven sent chance. But old Meadows was there. Nothing short of the complete dissolution of all matter could prevent that.

He looked over his glasses in surprise as Timothy came in.

"You!" Meadows exclaimed, and put a file away. "I thought you gave your notice."

"I did, sir, but—I—er—have the feeling that I was perhaps a little hasty. I wouldn't like to leave you in the lurch."

"I see." Meadows sat down and ran a finger over his mouth. Not a word about the amazing morning. Either he had not noticed it, or if he had, he refused to be budged from his habitual equanimity.

"It occurred to me that solicitor's clerks are hard to get—at least with my qualifications," Timothy hurried on. "So naturally I—"

"Not as hard to get as you think, Brown," Meadows interrupted. "I started a new clerk this morning. At the moment he is in the strong room looking up the deeds on that case of Milverton-v-Crookshank, which you—er—somewhat neglected."

Timothy blinked.

"So there it is," Meadows shrugged. "You gave your notice and I accepted it. I appreciate your wanting to help but it is no longer necessary."

"No—" Timothy's voice was dull. "Well, thank you, Mr. Meadows."

He crept out of the office, re-donned his hat and coat, and departed. This time he was no longer under any illusion. He had finished with law, as far as this firm was concerned. Only thing for it seemed to be to follow out his original plan and have that interview with Foster.

Moodily he returned to the street, and instantly became conscious of the weirdness of everything. It was like stepping into the midst of a partial eclipse. He glanced above, saw the ebony star-dusted sky, and shuddered. If ever a man had put his foot in it, he had! Just the same he had got to go on living, and, there was a chance that Foster might not have the scientific acumen to link up the dust destroyer with the present circumstances. If that proved to be the case the royalty cheque would still be forthcoming.

Timothy hurried on, his scruples thrown overboard, and presently, gained the enormous edifice of the Kleen

Sweep Company. It looked as though it had only been built a few hours, so impeccably clean were the collonades and windows. Within the great entrance hall the lights were burning with intense brilliance and a commissionaire moved calmly as though black skies and a total absence of dust were quite commonplace.

In three minutes Timothy was again in the presence of the overpowering Foster. "I'm a little late, I'm afraid," he apologized. "The—the extraordinary circumstances this morning delayed me."

"Mmmm," Foster acknowledged, which might have meant anything. "As a matter of fact, Mr. Brown, I am afraid I have something of a shock for you. I handed over your plans and details to my scientific experts at a late hour last night, so I could have their report in time for our interview this morning. They tell me that your dust-destroyer is much too dangerous a commodity to be offered to the public."

"Dangerous!" Timothy laughed unconvincingly. "But that's absurd! You saw for yourself how—"

"I have also seen what's happened since, Mr. Brown." Foster jerked his untidy head towards the window. "For your information, the conditions reigning this morning are caused by nothing less than your infernal dust destroyer! You are not a scientist, Mr. Brown: you're a madman!"

Timothy got a hold on himself. "Now just a minute, Mr. Foster! Where on earth did you get the idea that my dust destroyer caused this strange phenomenon of sun and sky? It couldn't!"

"It could, and it has. Expert physicists have already been saying over the radio and TV that the cause of our present strange conditions is the mysterious removal of dust, which has its centre somewhere in east London. Detector equipment is now at work endeavouring to trace possible vibratory waves which have caused dust to be annihilated."

"That's a waste of time, anyhow," Timothy said bitterly. "My instrument has not been used since I demonstrated it to you last night—"

"Then you agree it is responsible?"

"I suppose so," Timothy muttered. "But I never guessed a thing like this would happen. It's chain reaction. There is dust everywhere in the world, so as one dust molecule is destroyed it affects the next, with tremendous rapidity. In the end these conditions will travel all over the planet, I suppose."

"And you sit there and calmly admit the fact!" Foster exclaimed.

"What else do you expect me to do?"

"Find a solution to it, and damned quick! Tell the world what you've done and let the scientists get to work trying to unravel the mess you've created."

Timothy hesitated. "I can't see that it's such a mess. We want to be rid of dust, don't we? It's a curse and a menace wherever it lies. If the only price for it is a black sky and stars in the daytime I don't see it matters."

"Listen to me," Foster said deliberately. "News has been given over the radio and TV that up to now, since dawn anyway when this phenomenon was first noticed, there have been nearly five thousand deaths in London alone. Most of them were brought about by panic, and others by accidents, chiefly in the dense shadows. If it spreads all over the world, as seems inevitable, I shudder to think how many deaths will finally be attributable to you! Get the truth off your chest, man, and let scientists take the responsibility! As for our deal, it's right off! Here are your sketches back—"

Timothy took them slowly.

"And good morning," Foster added curtly.

Timothy hardly remembered reaching the street again. He was in a complete daze. At one fell swoop, it appeared, he had lost everything. When he arrived back home Elsie would have plenty to say: his life would be unbearable. The memory of his earlier scientific experiment which had blown up the house had not yet been lived down: now that he had succeeded in blackening the sky and throwing away his living as well there would be no limit to her derision.

Somehow the situation had to be faced, and while he tried to think how best to act things were happening in all parts of the city—and even beyond it as the black sky relentlessly crept onwards like an inky tide.

Religious revivalists were having a field day at every street corner, parading with hastily conceived banners exhorting the populace to declare its sins before the voice of Judgment spoke. In more sane paths the scientists were at work, all other tasks abandoned, striving to analyze the scientific riddle that had descended. So far there was no definite information to go on since Jacob Foster had not said a word about the dust destroyer for fear he himself might be involved.

Out in the streets there were countless collisions due to the utter blackness of the shadows. In areas overhung by tall buildings, buses and motor cars crashed into each other, the surviving drivers declaring that the blinding headlights of oncoming traffic had completely dazzled them. Collisions between pedestrians were almost as frequent and the hospitals had the busiest morning for years.

Towards half past ten, as the black sky remained unchanged, a deputation visited Greenwich Observatory. The curator was sympathetic, but vague. He admitted that he had no idea what had caused the phenomenon. The only explanation, in his opinion, was that by some unexplained means all the processes of refraction and diffusion had suddenly become set at naught, perhaps through the agency some new gas in outer space through which Earth, following her orbit, was passing.

Reporters were quick to get hold of this information and in consequence special scare editions of the newspapers appeared on the streets before noon with the comforting headlines:

EARTH IN DANGER OF DESTRUCTION

After this followed flesh-creeping descriptions of the fate liable to overtake humanity before long. Many hundreds more people put an end to themselves and a general panic would probably have set in but for the fact that the Greenwich curator himself spoke over the radio and television and explained the real facts—that he had only theorized on a possibility and that there was no direct evidence as yet.

Back at home Timothy kept in touch with the changing scene, listening to the news or buying newspapers as they came out. Elsie had not said anything at all in response to his tale of woe. Instead she had only looked, and now she was maintaining an icy silence, her mouth set hard.

"At least they can't blame me," Timothy said, towards three in the afternoon.

"Who can't?" Elsie asked bluntly. She was sprawled at her ease, accustomed somewhat to the change of conditions.

"The authorities and the scientists. They're looking into the problem, as I told you, and trying to trace its source. They'll never do it. Chain reaction has no source: it just is."

Elsie sniffed. "Whatever your faults, Timothy. I always believed you to be a man of honour. How you can slink there with all this tragedy going on is beyond me!"

"What do you suggest I should do? Go out and yell to the public that I did it? Realize what would happen if I did? I'd be locked up for life. Then what would you do?"

"As a matter of fact I'm wondering at this very moment what I'm going to do. You've lost your job; we've no money coming in, and obviously we can't go on living on our capital forever."

"I'll find something, don't worry. I—"

Timothy stopped and gave an uneasy glance as there came a steady ringing at the flat door. He hesitated for a moment then got to his feet. When he opened the door he saw two men, both in mackintoshes and soft hats, regarding him steadily. One of them carried a mahogany case by a strap slung over his shoulder.

"Metropolitan Police," said the taller of the two. "I have the authority to search your premises, sir—" He held out a buff-coloured form.

"Search the premises?" Timothy repeated blankly. "What the devil do you think I am—a criminal?"

The question was not answered. Instead the men strode past him and into the living room. The man with the mahogany case opened its lid and studied a dial like a clock-face within. Timothy could see a red needle swinging gently.

"Over there, somewhere," said the shorter man finally.

His companion nodded and glanced at Timothy. "Mind if I take a look at your bedroom, sir?"

"I mind very much! Who the devil are you? What do you want?"

"The source of a dangerous electrical disturbance which has caused the phenomenon in the city today. It's as simple as that."

"You don't suppose that has anything to do with me, do you?" Timothy snapped.

"I'm only doing my duty, sir," the tall one replied patiently. "Our instruments in the detector van outside have traced a peculiar electrical vibration to this spot, and this instrument double-checks it. The source of the vibration is only a yard or two away now—in that bedroom there."

"Oh," Timothy muttered, and gave Elsie a glance.

"Well, why don't you tell them?" she asked bluntly. "It might make things easier for you."

"Easier for me! Dammit, one would think I'd committed a murder, or something. All right," Timothy added, as the two men studied him, "I'll get the thing you're looking for, but it won't do you a scrap of good."

He went into the bedroom and returned with the heavy steel deed box in which he kept his precious gadget. Flinging back the lid he motioned to the instrument inside.

"All yours," he said bitterly. "Some use it was for me to get a bright idea."

The men looked at the gadget but they did not touch it. Instead they consulted the detector, nodded to each other, and then closed down the lid of the box.

"Better come along with us, sir," the taller one said. "The Physical Research laboratory will want an explanation. Don't misunderstand me: this is not in the nature of an arrest, or anything like that."

Timothy sighed, gave Elsie a dubious glance, and went for his hat and coat. He was taken in the detector van to the headquarters of the Physical Research laboratory and at length shown into an office where four or five men were assembled, studying charts upon which flags had been staked.

"I think we've nailed the cause of the trouble, gentlemen," said Timothy's tall escort. "This gentleman will explain, and in this box is the instrument we found."

The middle-aged man seated at the desk motioned to a chair and Timothy slowly sat down, glancing from one face to the other. He noticed they were all intelligent looking men—and worried-looking, too.

"Your name, sir?" enquired the man at the desk.

"Timothy Brown."

"Thank you, Mr. Brown. I am Dr. Henderson, in charge of the scientific branch of the metropolitan police. These gentlemen are all scientists."

Timothy looked at them and smiled weakly. Dr. Henderson's sharp grey eyes travelled to the deed box.

"What have you in this box, Mr. Brown?"

"An invention, and I see no reason why I should be cal upon to explain it. It's my personal property."

The grey eyes moved and fixed on Timothy's. He felt himself wilt before their intensity.

"Mr. Brown, you must be aware, in common with everybody else in London, of the astounding things that have been observed since dawn. The public demands an explanation and the scientists, en masse, have been struggling to find the answer to the mystery. We believe we have—now. Open this box, please."

Timothy had no alternative. Immediately the scientists gathered around and gazed in some astonishment at the Gadget as Timothy brought it forth.

"What is it?" Dr. Henderson asked politely.

"A dust destroyer. When switched on it 'collapses' molecules of dust—"

"Be more explicit," Henderson ordered. "Every detail if you please."

Surrounded by science and the law Timothy meekly explained the whole thing, taking some comfort from thought that the patent he had filed protected him.

"Well, gentlemen?" Henderson asked the assembled scientists.

"This is the answer, sir," one of them replied. "It started chain-reaction in dust molecules, and the thing has just gone on and on."

"That's it," Timothy agreed. "But believe me when I say had not the least idea that such a thing would happen. As far as I could tell the influence of the instrument should have ceased from the moment it was switched off. But I must have been wrong."

"Desperately, tragically wrong!" Henderson snapped, getting to his feet. "You should never have attempted an experiment like this, Mr. Brown, without first consulting experienced scientists. As things are you have precipitated a crisis. It is going to take science all its time to undo the tragedy you have created."

Timothy was silent. All he had wanted to do was produce the most wonderful dust destroyer in the world, and in return he was in this mess.

"I am not sure," Henderson mused, "under what classification your offence comes. "I shall leave that to the normal police department. You will leave your instrument here, Mr. Brown, and return home with these two police officers for all notes and formulae connected with this invention of ours."

"You can have them now." Timothy fumbled in his inside pocket. Everything was there, just as Foster had handed them to him earlier in the day.

"Thanks," Henderson said briefly. "And don't leave town."

Timothy departed, completely bewildered and not a little scared. In the office he had vacated the scientists looked at one another, then the chief physicist amongst them picked up Timothy's formula and studied it.

"Without doubt," he muttered at length, "the man's a genius! Trouble is this genius hasn't taken the trouble to weigh up consequences. He just gave birth to his brainchild, for ill or good—and now we get a result like this!"

He glanced towards the window where the black sky of the afternoon was dusted with brilliant stars.

"The point is—" Henderson began, then he broke off as a voices spoke from a loudspeaker.

"Dark area spreading at same speed. All London is now involved and the effect is spreading in an ever-widening circle. People have been warned of the approach of the tide and must make their own preparations. General evacuation is not advised since there is no actual danger from the dark area, except perhaps in shadows. Everywhere dust is fast vanishing. Stand by—"

CHAPTER 3

Nature Transformed

"No actual danger!" repeated the chief physicist sourly. "You hear that? So says a high and mighty Government official who hasn't the least idea of the gravity of the situation. Why, if this business goes on almost anything can happen! And from the expressions on the faces of you gentlemen here I even begin to think that none of you appreciate what we're in for, either."

"Whatever we might be in for mustn't be allowed to happen," Henderson said curtly. "This dust chain reaction must be stopped. Call all the help you need. Get the best scientists in the world."

The scientists looked at one another; then the chief physicist said: "Have "I permission to take this instrument and the plans? We'll need to make an intensive study to solve the business. Chain reaction isn't new, of course, and there are ways of checking it—only Brown's been so infernally clever in limiting his vibration to one particular form of molecule it's going to be a stinger to solve."

"Take everything you need and spare no expense," Henderson ordered. "The public is relying on us to bring back blue skies and normal life—"

Easily said, but not so easily done—and the scientists knew it. Meanwhile, the cause of all the trouble was on his way back home, wandering moodily through the inky shadows and blinding sunshine. As he went he reviled the fact that he had a streak of genius in his make-up, which had got him into the worst pickle of his life. It seemed that the only time worth having would be night, when the skies would be black, anyway.

Timothy was not alone in his contemplations of the phenomenon, either. The man-in-the-street, suitably primed by now with the scare newspapers and media reports, was worried. Business was already becoming jerky. In cars, trains, buses, and tube the one topic of conversation was the black sky and mysterious disappearance of dust. It was remarkable, too, how incredibly well washed and neat everybody looked, from the grimiest labourer to the proprietress of a beauty salon. Dust was on the march, from skin, clothes, streets, buildings—everywhere. Even the slums, rotten with the accumulated dirt of years, were bright and resplendent, something for the train travellers to gaze upon in stunned wonder.

It was towards teatime when Timothy returned home, and the sun had just set at the close of the most amazing day in Earth's history. Indeed Timothy had lingered to watch that sunset from a clear vantage point. There had been something sinister about that blue white ball, with its attendant corona and prominences, sinking down until the horizon had cleanly bisected it, and finally swallowed it. No twilight, no pink flush, no clouds. Just night—as dark as the tomb and glittering now with multitudes of stars which had never been seen before.

Timothy was glad to get into the flat again, to warmth, and a bright light—yes, even to Elsie. She had prepared tea but seemed surprised at his return.

"Thought you might have gone for good," she said, tossing down her woman's paper. "Kettle will soon boil. What did they say to you?"

"Nothing. Or almost nothing." Timothy took off his hat and coat. "They told me I should have asked experts before setting my invention to work. That's a good one! Had I done that they'd have pinched the idea and that would have been that!"

"Instead of which you've blacked out the sky, lost your job, and not got a cent for your great idea! Will you never learn sense, Timothy? You should have stuck to your affadavits."

Timothy did not answer, chiefly because he realized Elsie was probably right for once. Moodily he switched on the radio, listened for a moment to a tale of woe, then switched off again. Eventually tea was ready, and he settled down.

"The point is," Elsie said, for about the sixth time, "what are you going to do? We can't live on fresh air."

"Fresh isn't the word for it," Timothy replied absently. "I noticed it just after the sun had dipped. It went as cold as during a total eclipse—and it's getting colder. There'll be a record frost tonight, you'll see."

"Not unusual so near to Christmas, is it?"

"This is different. No clouds are blanketing in the warmth of the day, such as it was, and therefore the thermometer just plummets down. Be like that as long as the sky remains as it is. Seasons may even change."

Elsie stared. "The seasons! Great heavens, you don't mean to say this business is going to continue? You don't mean we're never going to see a blue sky again?"

"Unless we find a way to undo chain-reaction that is exactly the prospect," Timothy answered. "And don't blame me for it, either. I only started an unusual law of Nature in operation: not my fault what transpires after that."

"This isn't like you," Elsie said, surprisingly. Timothy looked at her, struck by the odd tone in her voice.

"Not like me? How d'you mean?"

"I mean that when there's a problem somewhere you usually set to work to solve it. Not necessarily a scientific one—but a problem of any kind. This time you're lying down on the job."

"Not I! I just happen to know when I'm licked. It's up to the scientists now."

"Why should it be? It's your pigeon, isn't it? I can't understand your attitude. You hand over that invention of yours—"

"Because I had to."

"Never mind about that. You hand it over and calmly leave the scientists to work out your notes—all of which you must know far better than they do. Surely the problem is yours, Timothy? Since you started the trouble it seems to me it's your job to put it right."

"But I keep telling you! I can't! I don't know how. I'm a solicitor's clerk, remember—"

"You told me you'd become a scientist, so act like one! Do you think any of the scientists you've seen so far could have invented your dust destroyer?"

"No!" Timothy replied with conviction. "It was the sort of scientific inspiration which is only given to the few."

"Very well, then. Since you are unique you're probably the only man on the face of the Earth who can undo the trouble. Heaven knows, Timothy, we're always bickering at each other but we do know each other's capabilities.

You tell me I'm a good cook: I say you're a good scientist, but too heedless of consequences. Start thinking what to do about this trouble. Reverse what you've done."

Timothy gazed blankly for a full fifteen seconds. It had been worth turning the sky black to hear Elsie's real opinion of him.

"Why not?" he breathed, a gleam in his eye. "There's an antidote for every poison if you can only find it, just as there is a counteractive for every vibration. Maybe I can stop chain-reaction."

"Since you've no job on your hands you may as well. If you don't there won't be jobs for anybody."

Timothy stirred his tea absently. "First," he said, "I must make a change and clear the mental attic. I think we should go to the cinema."

"Cinema! What in the world for? They may not even be open as things are."

"Course they'll be open! Everything's going on as usual even though circumstances are somewhat changed. I can't settle down to any serious thinking without a rest first."

Elsie sighed and gave it up. Not that she objected to going to the cinema: it would be a change for a while, anyway—so an hour later found she and Timothy in the stalls. They had things almost to themselves since there were not above half a dozen people in the place—which was a pity, Elsie thought, because the show was quite a good one judging by its reviews.

It was immediately noticeable that the seats were bright red plush, a fact that Timothy and Elsie had never known in all the years they had been patrons of the Regal.

"Not new, just clean;" Timothy murmured, as Elsie looked about her on the spotless walls and grime-free ceiling.

"People have been saved a terrible lot of expense thanks to that invention of yours," she commented. "If only you hadn't been so wholesale about it!"

"Not my fault. Chain reaction is just one of those things."

Elsie said no more, and presently the performance started.

Timothy, despite trying, was not nearly as interested in the film as he was in the fact that between the projector and the screen there was no trace whatever of a beam. And the air was light and pure and totally free from dust.

Timothy, for his part, could not become interested in the rugged Western hero walking tight-lipped and un-armed down the main street of some mythical gold-rush town: his mind was going over the equations for his dust destroyer, juggling with the mathematics in a desperate endeavour to discover some means of undoing the cataclysm he had started.

He was still thoughtful when the show had ended and he and Elsie walked out into the amazing night. The air was intensely cold and seemed to crackle in its crispness. The hooting of tugs on the Thames, the whistle of trains in the stations and yards, came clearly above the deeper, more compelling note of the general traffic.

"Why should everything be louder?" Elsie asked, as she and Timothy walked slowly home.

"Because dust forms an invisible screen in the ordi-nary way, which very slightly deflects sound waves. Just as you don't hear a person speaking as clearly through a handkerchief as in the normal way. The air is utterly free of any deflection and dust."

"That must be a good thing in spite of what the scientists say," Elsie insisted. "After all, the dustless air of the mountains is recommended for people suffering from lung complaints, so surely this flawless air we have now must be doing good?"

"I hope so," Timothy answered dubiously, not at all sure what effect his spreading dust-destroying wave was having.

Elsie glanced at him, but he did not explain further—so they went on walking and listening in wonder to a myriad sounds they had never heard before. And in the Physical Laboratory the scientists still toiled desperately to find the solution to the riddle.

By midnight London, for once, was comparatively peaceful. The astounding change in everything had driven most people to bed far earlier than usual, but for many there was no sleep. Even the quietest regions were alive with noises that had never previously been detected. Thousands heard Big Ben chime the hours across the city, even those in regions that had never heard him there before. The air was still, and an apparent magnetic conductor of sound waves. Vast and inexplicable things were happening as Timothy Brown's dust-atom destruction spread with relentless speed.

The following morning the sky was still black. Once more there was an incredible sunrise of a blazing, blue-white ball shedding its pitiless brilliance on a panicky populace. And with this morning there began the great exodus as all those who could afford to leave the city began to jam the railway stations for trains departing to other parts of the country where the skies were still blue and the sun shone normally. The confusion was appalling and nobody seemed willing to heed the information that the black area was spreading steadily and must, finally, encompass the whole country and perhaps the world.

In a different sphere were the astronomers. They were at the close of a long night of observations, and with the impartiality of true scientists they gleefully announced to the Press that, thanks to the cleanness of the air, they had been able to log sixteen new distant galaxies—which they had never known existed—and also additional dwarf planets at the limits of the solar system. Indeed, in the light of the changed conditions it was generally agreed that astronomy as a whole must undergo drastic revision as all known star charts had become obsolete.

Strangest discovery of all, for the average man and woman, was that despite the intense coldness of the night there was no frost and no dew, simply because there were no dust-motes for either condition to seize upon. Strange, mystical transformation of Nature, indeed!

And so to the commercial world, the lifeblood of the country. Here there was trouble indeed, particularly with the great firm of Zenith Dyers and Cleaners. The managing director thereof called an extraordinary meeting of shareholders and gave them the simple facts.

"Bankruptcy, in a few months is the prospect for us unless conditions return to normal. It must have become evident to you, as to everybody else, that our particular form of business is doomed to become obsolete. The veriest tramp in the gutter is wearing clothes as clean as though new, so what chance do we stand? Though the changed conditions have only been in existence for something like twenty-four hours I am informed from all our branches that custom has ceased completely. It will take perhaps a month to clear up back orders—which have automatically been cleaned for us! What happens after that? Do we close now and make sure of what capital we have, or do we hang on in the hope that things might improve?"

The result of consultation and voting was that the Zenith Dyers and Cleaners would hang on a while longer and hope for the best; but this was not the case with the Kleen Sweep Brush Company. Jacob Foster was determined to close, and said so bluntly to his fellow directors.

"But why?" one of them demanded. "These conditions may be cleared up at any minute. The media keep on telling us that the scientists will solve the problem—"

"I don't believe they ever will," Foster retorted. "I know the man who caused all this trouble, and he told me frankly that he knew of no way to stop it. Since he brought about the chaos he is obviously the one possible man to find a way to cure it, and since even he admits defeat where are we?"

"Who is he?" another director demanded. "What right has he to be hidden from public notice when a business like this has to be dealt with?"

"That," Foster said deliberately, "is not our concern. It might not do us any good to be linked with him. I tell you frankly gentlemen, that I was on the point of buying exclusive rights in his dust destroyer, the very thing that has brought about the present conditions, therefore it would hardly be prudent to be linked with him now in any way."

"I don't agree," said another. "Why should we give up one of the finest vacuum cleaning businesses in the world? Perhaps this lunatic can save us? Maybe we can scare him into it?"

"I doubt it. I think he has a one-track scientific mind. He invented this infernal device of his, but as for knowing how to cure the condition it has brought about—" Foster gave a hopeless shrug.

There was a grim, troubled silence. Outside the window the flood of unmasked sunlight blazed down on a spotless city of eldritch shadows.

"Whatever you gentlemen may decide to do, I'm pulling out," Foster said finally. "We're finished, along with all others in this line of business."

Just about which time the street cleaners of London were ordered to cease work. There was no dust to clean up, and other refuse could easily be taken care of by a skeleton staff.

Thousands of char women throughout the city got their marching orders on the second day of the Blackness, as it had now become popularly called. No floors needed sweeping, no offices needed dusting. So into the discard went thousands of women who could ill afford to lose the little they had been earning.

Hard after them came the window cleaners, both those who were self-employed and the employees of large combines in charge of London's mightiest buildings. For them, too, work had ceased. In all the infinities of glass in London there was not a smear, not a trace of defilement. Shop windows, indeed, looked as though there were no glass intervening at all.

Few could have foreseen how much unemployment the destruction of dust was producing. After the office cleaners and window cleaners came the employees of the big building-cleaning firms. There was no need any more for armies of men to crawl about on scaffolding and scrub the filthy faces of the older buildings. Old and new edifices alike were as bright as the day they had been built. The only signs of age were in erosion, which of course had nothing to do with the annihilation of dust. And on the heels of these workers came the laundry employees—tens of thousands of them; employees of the big public services retained specially for the cleaning of public vehicles; the brush factory employees; the vacuum-cleaner salesmen and clerical staffs of the firms concerned—the whole great army which had, before the meddling of Timothy Brown, devoted itself to keeping the city and the person spotless.

Employment Exchanges began to bulge with overflowing queues on that second morning of the Darkness. Restless men and women of all ages muttered and growled amongst themselves under the star-ridden sky. Files of waiting people stretched out into streets, which looked as though they had been abraded with acres of sandpaper. Here, in these swelling throngs, were the beginnings of grim trouble, for inevitably the structure of social life must fall apart as one vital element of it was removed.

The scientists still laboured, as they had throughout the night. By noon on the second day they had arrived at the conclusion that they were beaten.

"No answer to this one," declared the chief physicist, as Henderson, haggard from a sleepless night, came in to observe progress "Brown has got this formula of his absolutely air-tight He's created a vibration that destroys dust atoms completely The only saving grace—if we can call it that—is that he was ingenious enough to limit the annihilation to dust atoms alone. Had he tampered with the basic structure of other forms of matter, which vibrate at a different wavelength, the whole world would be falling to pieces around us right now."

"Are you sure it isn't?" Henderson asked bitterly. "The end of dust can mean the end of civilization—in time."

The scientists were silent, appreciating the truth of his statement. Then he went on briefly, "The trouble is still spreading at a uniform rate, consistent with the speed of chain reaction and radiating in a circle from the original core which started things. The radius now involves the edges of Bedford, Buckingham, Sussex, Kent, and Essex. At the present speed the whole of the country may be involved within a week. What are we to do, gentlemen?"

"Might see if this fellow Brown has any suggestions," the physicist replied. "It's conceivable he may be able to reverse the system somehow, though I doubt it. I'd suggest you have him come over, sir."

Accordingly, Timothy Brown arrived in the presence of the scientists towards half past ten. He was unshaven, looked incredibly tired, and as usual had an air of bewilderment.

"Nothing for us to do, Mr. Brown, but throw this whole problem in your lap," Henderson said bluntly. "These trained scientists are stumped in trying to find a way to stop the trouble you started."

"So am I," Timothy muttered, sitting down and gazing dully before him.

"But you must have some kind of idea!" Henderson insisted.

"Theory is no use without practice, is it?" Timothy demanded. "Look at me, my friends! I've been working all night on a theory, only to find it didn't work. One thing I do know quite definitely—"

The scientists leaned forward expectantly.

"We cannot stop chain reaction, as such."

"That we already know," Henderson retorted.

"But it might be possible to segregate the trouble," Timothy finished absently.

The physicist looked at his colleagues and frowned. "Segregate it? It isn't possible to isolate the destruction of dust molecules now the thing has started. Dust is everywhere and the vibratory wave you sent forth has caused one atom to touch off another everywhere there is dust. How do you propose to segregate that?"

"I suggest we divide the dust atoms which are as yet untouched from the area which is disintegrating." Timothy made a vague motion. "Like they do when there's a forest fire. They burn away parts ahead of the fire to stop it travelling. Something on that principle."

"I don't see how," the chief physicist confessed worriedly.

"Neither do I—yet, but there must be some way of doing it. I have a hazy notion of an instrument capable of exerting a negative effect on the disintegrating area. Like a screen, or safety curtain. If we could do that and isolate the disturbance—"

"We still would not improve the area that has been rendered dustless," Henderson snapped. "Suppose we put up such a theoretical screen at this moment and stopped the process spreading throughout its entire radius, what then? The rest of the world would be saved, yes, but what about the part already affected?"

"We can restore it," Timothy said, as though he regarded this as merely a side issue. "Don't you see that when the last of the dust atoms on the 'disintegrative' side of the screen has exploded the trouble is done with?

It can't carry on because it has been isolated and there is nothing left to disintegrate. When that moment happens we cut off the screen and the dust and wind currents from the unaffected regions will flow into the area that has been deprived. Within a few weeks everything would return to normal. The disintegrative business could never happen again without that vibration being used. Which reminds me: what have you done with my dust destroyer?"

"Taken it to pieces," replied the chief physicist. "We had to do that to gain a knowledge of its workings. When things are straightened out you can have it back."

"Keep it," Timothy said, shuddering. "I never want to see it again."

Henderson, who had been plunged in thought, said slowly: "I believe that you really have an idea there, Mr. Brown—in that disruptive screen. Can you work it out? We freely admit that we can't because we don't exactly know the original electrical basis of your dust destroying vibration."

"I can work it out if I am left in peace and not called over here every five minutes. The trouble is I can't concentrate as strongly as I'd like to because I'm not sure how I stand with the law. What am I? A criminal, a menace to public safety, a lunatic, or what? I've got to know if I am likely to be arrested."

"You won't be that," Henderson reassured him. "I've had that side of the matter over with the Assistant Commissioner and there is no legal clause upon which we can nail you. The whole thing was a scientific accident and you can't be held directly responsible. Even if you could I'd veto any moves against you because you are the only man who can possibly get us out of the dilemma."

Timothy got to his feet, a new light in his eye. "That being so I'll throw everything I've got into turning this business back in its tracks. The moment I have something I'll get in touch with you."

When he had gone the scientists looked at Henderson.

"You really trust him to save civilization?" the chief physicist asked in wonder.

Henderson shrugged. "What alternative have I? What alternative have any of us?"

"Just the same," the physicist said, "we'll go on experimenting in case our eccentric friend doesn't find the answer."

Timothy, though, really had something, if only he could get it into proper focus in his mind. He felt tolerably certain that he could master the problem: it was time that was the gnawing factor. The disintegrative process was spreading at an alarming and steady pace, conforming in velocity to all the laws of physics, and if he had not solved how to make a 'segregating screen' by the time the last atom of dust had been destroyed all hope would be gone. Everything relied on having one remaining patch of dust, one scrap of blue sky, one cloud where dust remained.

Small wonder that he was troubled and thoughtful when he arrived back home again. Elsie, prosaically peeling potatoes, looking at him briefly.

"Now what?" she asked.

"Quite enough. The scientists are licked and they've passed the buck to me." Timothy threw down his hat and coat and warmed his hands at the gas fire. "It's an odd thought, Elsie, but I'm perhaps the only man who can save the world."

"I seem to think I mentioned that last evening when I told you to get a move on—or if I didn't I thought it."

"Gives one an odd feeling of limitless power," Timothy mused. "The teeming millions of this world all relying on me to save them. If I succeed I'll be one of the immortals of science, like I've always wanted to be. There'll be statues of me when I'm dead, maybe."

"Forget for the moment that you're a Napoleon, Timothy Brown, and realize one other factor! You caused the whole thing, so there won't be any praise if you cure it. People will just sigh in relief and then be after your blood for scaring their wits out."

Timothy started and turned. "You really think so?"

"Yes." Elsie tossed a potato in the pan. "I've lived long enough to know human nature."

"In that case there isn't much use in my trying to solve the mystery. I don't want kicking around after saving anybody."

"Now you listen to me—" Elsie pointed the potato peeler significantly. "The scientists have handed the business over to you to solve. If you don't you'll suffer a far worse fate at the hands of enraged people than if you did. Besides, you owe it to your conscience and to me to put matters right."

Timothy turned from the fire and threw himself on the sofa, drawing a writing pad to him.

"After this I'll be a scientist no more," he declared. "You get more kicks than a football! Now don't bother me. I've got to think."

He was not the only one doing some thinking, either. For instance, the head of the Metropolitan Water Board was distraught by a problem, so much so that he had called upon Henderson at the Physical Laboratory.

"Do I understand, Mr. Henderson, that our present black sky and dustless conditions are a freak of Nature?"

"One might call it that," Henderson admitted, thinking of the scientists sweating blood in the laboratory.

"Right. Up to now I have not heard any information which suggests the trouble might lift. I am responsible for the continued water supply of this city, so what am I to tell people when they find water failing? It will, you know, if the sky remains like this. No clouds, no rain. What's the answer?"

"Distillation of sea water," Henderson replied, at which the water board chief laughed shortly.

"My dear sir, you are a scientist! You know just how much such a colossal project would cost."

"Certainly I know, but if the population has no other way of getting fresh water it will have to be done."

"Mr. Henderson, I'm uneasy. Your suggestion means that you have seen the possibility of the black sky remaining unchanged."

"One has to be prepared," Henderson said grimly. "We are struggling to solve the trouble, but we are only human. If we fail... Well, we'll take desperate measures then, with Government authority. Meantime, keep a constant watch on water conservation."

"I will," the water board man responded, mopping his forehead. "And I regret to say you've confirmed my worst fears."

Henderson was silent, and very soon afterwards he discovered that the water board man was only the first of a constant stream of public men and women wanting to know what was likely to happen. Most of these people had first contacted Whitehall and from there been directed to Henderson who 'had the matter in hand'—or at least fervently wished that he had.

The Minister for Agriculture was another who had the rain-bug in his bonnet. What was he to say to the farmers when they reported their crops were dying for lack of rain? What prospect was there of normalcy returning? Henderson gave guarded replies, which was all he could do in the circumstances.

By mid-afternoon he was wearied with questions and desperately hungry. He closed his offices after dispatching a special messenger to discover how Timothy Brown was faring with his attempts to solve the riddle. The messenger's response, half an hour later, made Henderson nearly drop his sandwich. Timothy Brown was reading a scientific adventure story in a boy's paper and didn't wish to be disturbed.

"Who the hell does he think he is?" he stormed, leaping up.

"I—I don't know, sir." The messenger was startled, looking very much like a Martian in his crash helmet and motorcycle kit. "But that's what he was doing and that was his message. I saw the paper he was reading."

"What was its name?"

"*Teenagers' Weekly*, sir. I take it myself sometimes. Some smashing yarns in it—"

"Get out!" Henderson spat; then wheeling round he went through the maze of spotless corridors to the main laboratory.

"News, sir?" asked the head physicist hopefully.

"No! At least not good news. I came to tell you to work harder than you've ever done. Brown's going to be no good to us. He's reading a teenage weekly or something and obviously isn't giving any attention to the problem in hand. Damnit, I've a mind to have him arrested."

"No," the physicist said, shaking his head. "It wouldn't do. He may have something but likes to relax while it jells in his mind. I do things like that."

Henderson turned a delicate purple. "Blast it, am I surrounded by lunatics?" he demanded. "This is no time to relax and let things jell! Look at that damned sky outside! Look at the string of people who are pestering me to know what we're up to and when the rain is going to start again! Get busy, the whole lot of you!"

He stormed out of the laboratory again and the scientists looked at one another.

"Just one of his moods," the physicist shrugged. "I never had any faith in Brown, anyway."

They could hardly be blamed for their reaction to Timothy Brown's strange behaviour; but then Timothy was not one of the common herd and therefore did things in an original way. Solicitor's clerk he might have been, but if anybody had had sufficient patience and insight they would have grasped that in Timothy there reposed the mind of a man equalling Edison, Marconi, and Baird in its tremendous grasp of scientific possibilities—but Timothy had not had a scientific education and therefore his ideas were untamed and dangerous. As for his reading a teenage thriller while Rome burned—and there were good reasons for that, too.

Elsie, unfortunately, took the same line as Henderson. She saw only a man sprawling on the sofa in front of the gas fire, a black sky outside, and heaven knew what in the immediate future. Though she had an inborn faith in his peculiar gifts she often found them submerged by immediate reactions—as at this moment as she laid the dinner table.

"Trying to solve this problem is one thing, Timothy, and I know I stung you into it—but there's still another bigger one. What do we do for money?"

Timothy grunted and went on reading his weekly.

"We can't go beyond three months." Elsie sucked her teeth pensively. "You'll have to find work and solve this black sky business at the same time."

Timothy slowly lowered his paper to the sofa and then struggled to his feet.

"For your edification, my dear," he said slowly, "I have under three months in which to solve this business. If I have not done it by then it means the end of every-thing. The end of you, of me, of all civilization."

"Does it?" Elsie looked at him stupidly. "I hadn't quite realized— But it can't be that bad. Only a black sky—"

"Only! Great heavens, woman, if that were the only thing I could take years over the job. It isn't, though: there are countless factors involved and the main one is loss of rain. No rain will ever fall again here until this trouble is righted. As water fails everything fails: it's as simple as that."

"And you sit and read a boys' paper!"

"Don't question what I'm doing, Elsie, I'm thinking. I may do lots of queer things before I'm finished. Any-how, it's time I had something to eat. Can't think without food."

"Then we live on our capital until—"

"Time is the factor! Time!"

CHAPTER 4

The Darkness spreads

Days passed: days of the black sky, sun, moon, and stars, and mankind, in England anyway, became more or less accustomed to the strangeness of everything. The deeper implications connected with the trouble did not occur to the average man and woman. They simply realized that they had their normal everyday jobs to do, and went on doing them, trusting to the scientists and the Government because they could do little else.

Those with money had already departed to more normal climes, but again they were forced on the move as the relentless Blackness kept on spreading—across the Atlantic to the west, and over the North Sea to Europe on the cast. Reports were constantly coming in of the sky turning grey, then brown, and at last ebony. Paris and Berlin were already involved, but on the western side, since the out-flowing circle of disintegration was of exact diameter, only the first half of the Atlantic had been involved. Seamen and airmen reported that moving from the dark area into the normal was like hurtling through pea-soup fog.

Realizing that something had to be done, at least until the problem was solved, the Governments of Paris and London set up a system of powerful floodlighting which served to relieve the shadows from their inky darkness. Immediately the accident rate began to drop.

It seemed strange, therefore, that in the middle of London, where even the soot-encrusted gargoyles now gleamed in the blinding sunshine, there should have appeared the first signs of a mysterious disease. It was the kind of trouble one would have connected with dust since it was a form of erysipelas—an intense skin irritation accompanied in its later stages by uncontrollable coughing, from which the victim invariably died.

Medical science was nonplussed. The victims who came into the hospitals were given every known treatment, without the least effect. How a disease, which seemed to have its origin in dirt, could possibly be so stubborn in a city which had been rendered utterly dustless, was something which had the best brains of Harley Street guessing. Henderson was consulted, but he could not answer the riddle, either. So the B.M.A. convened a meeting and ordered Timothy Brown to be present. He came—reluctantly.

"The disease is not very difficult to understand," he said, after he had heard the most harrowing details. "All human beings, no, matter how clean, are covered with a certain amount of dust, and the people who are falling victims are those upon whom the disintegration effect is having a latent reaction. The dust atoms upon the skin are being annihilated with consequent severe irritation. I assume the coughing bouts have something to do with it, but I don't know what."

"And the cure?" asked a famous dermatologist.

"There isn't one until dust returns, far as I know. I am not a medical man—"

Having said his piece Timothy Brown returned to the lair and worked once more on the equations and symbols, which had now accumulated into several good-sized notebooks. Elsie, when she returned from shopping, found him on the floor peering under the sofa, whilst around him lay cushions, papers, books, and a general confusion of odds and ends.

"What on earth are you doing?" she demanded, by now heartily sick of Timothy constantly at home—for it meant that he could always watch how much work she did.

"Looking for my boys' weekly," he retorted. "Where have you put it? What on earth do you want to tidy the place up for the moment my back's turned?"

Elsie swallowed. "That's a good one—you who are ways complaining I never keep the place as you want it. I took the opportunity to straighten things a bit whilst you were at the B.M.A. I just couldn't turn around for stuff."

"Where," Timothy asked deliberately, straightening up, "Is that boys' weekly?"

"I burned it, along with all those other fool papers and catalogues you'd stored up. Since dust has gone we may as well have the place clear as well."

Timothy stared as though he had not heard a word. When he did speak at last it was in a whisper.

"You burned that magazine?"

"Why—yes." Elsie looked uncertain. "Don't stare at me like that, Timothy, you're giving me the creeps—"

"Great heavens, woman, you've probably destroyed last hope of saving civilization!" he yelled in blind fury. "I'd almost got the answer! In fact I'd have it at the moment if you'd only keep your confounded hands to yourself!"

"But—but how could that boys' paper possibly help? You only whiled away your time reading it—"

"I didn't!" Timothy screamed, banging the table. "I didn't! In one of those stories, called 'Hell on Earth', there was the basis of the solution to our present difficulties. The author probably was not aware of it himself, but when I read it I realized that his formula, though fictional, had the basis of practical possibility. My original dust-destroyer was only the offshoot of a story I once read— That author conceived an answer upon which I could have worked—and you burn it!"

"I'm most dreadfully sorry," Elsie muttered. "But how could I possibly know?"

Timothy was hurrying into his hat and coat. "I've got to have another copy immediately. If I can't do that I must contact the author himself and see if he has a carbon copy or something."

"Isn't he going to think things?"

"Why should he? He doesn't know who I am. He'll mistake me for a rabid fan."

Timothy departed in a hurry and in fifteen minutes was pounding up the stairs of Teenage Publications Limited, a back street affair without, it appeared, a very great financial backing. The editor had lack-lustre eyes and deathly pale face. He gazed in some astonishment as Timothy burst into his solitary, manuscript-littered office.

"Sorry to bother you," Timothy apologized. "I would like a back number of the 'Weekly'—August tenth, last year."

The editor smiled hopelessly. "So would I!"

"This is serious! I must have it."

"Quite impossible—sorry. Be only too glad to oblige if I could, but I have to work to a very small paper quota and all my numbers are sold out as fast as they appear."

Timothy sat down. "In that paper you ran a story called 'Hell on Earth'—a yam about a man who decided to clean up the dirt of a northern industrial town with some kind of vibration instrument. When he failed to do it he put the instrument in reverse and made things dirty again."

"Uh-huh," the editor admitted tiredly. "That was a good yarn, and I wish I could find more like it. But why so interested? You're hardly a teenager."

"That's beside the point. Have you any readers who may have back numbers?"

"No idea. Possibly; but I haven't the time to find out."

"Only one thing for it then: I must contact the author himself. Where do I find him?"

"St. James's Cemetery. He died two months ago."

"He what!" Timothy leapt up in horror.

"That so unusual? He was getting on a bit anyway, in spite of his teenage style. After all," the editor finished, looking suspicious, "no story could be that important. And old Daunton Neil was no Shakespeare, believe me!"

There was a stunned look on Timothy's face as he grappled with the situation. At last he asked another question.

"Any idea what happened to his effects? Has he a widow who might have them?"

"He was a bachelor. What happened to his stuff I don't know, but I can take a pretty good guess. There'd be no copy of that story, I'm sure. He never made any of the yarns he did. Once when I had a fire and asked for a quick carbon from him he had none. He rewrote the story from memory."

"I see," Timothy muttered, realizing that the well had run dry. "Thanks anyway—"

He departed slowly and left a much-mystified man behind. On his way back through the streets Timothy felt very much like killing Elsie. For months she had finnicked about and refused to tidy anything; then when she had suddenly started she'd destroyed the very thing he needed. There was only one solution, and a faint one: advertise for a back number. So he turned back to the editor and secured his promise to run an advertisement in the next issue. He also put an advertisement in the local press and then went home to moodily survey his very much unbalanced equations. Elsie had no need to ask him about his mission.

"If only my memory were good enough to remember!" he muttered, clenching his fist.

Elsie looked at him from the safety of the other end of the room.

"Something's just beginning to dawn on me," she said slowly. "You're not a brilliant scientist at all! You're not even an inventor. You pinch the idea from somebody else and then make it work."

"If that isn't invention, what is?" Timothy snapped.

"It's not invention as I understand it. You should conceive the whole thing out of nothing."

"Don't be ridiculous! No inventor ever did that. Everything is an offshoot of everything else. I simply have the kind of mind which, when I see a thing in theory, I can turn it into practical use. That's why I'm stuck now without that paper. If it doesn't come to light it's the finish."

"And until it does come to light what are you going to do?"

"Try and remember what I read. If only time were not such a desperate factor in the whole business!"

Elsie was silent, wondering what the bigwigs of Whitehall and the scientific department would have said had they known everything now depended on a boys' paper!

Actually, behind the scenes, a good deal was going on. The menace of the spreading black sky and total absence of cloud had already produced the obvious prospect of no rain, so the ministers of H.M. government began to confer with the scientists and the water engineers to discover what must be done. Henderson's original scheme for distillation of seawater was given a long and sympathetic study. Despite the enormous cost it would involve, and the demands upon labour, it might in the end be the only solution.

"Granting," Henderson said, "that there are enough people left alive to handle the project if it comes to it."

"Left alive?" one of the delegates asked.

"I'm referring to this disease which is mowing people down. There's no use trying to hide the fact that hundreds are dying every day. In a month or two that is going make a big gap in the population, and that's assuming the trouble doesn't get any worse. To the best of my belief it will be as progressive as the Darkness itself. And what does the B.M.A. do? Nothing."

"Because they can't," said a Cabinet minister. "It's something which never happened before."

"We don't only face failure of water," said a scientist. "Crops and food are automatically involved. I suggest that a rationing system be devised immediately. With no hope yet of solving our difficulties it's the only sane course."

So they argued and suggested, and planned. And in another part of London Timothy Brown sweated and strained his memory uselessly. Day by day he heard of the steady advance of the Darkness and groaned as he computed how much nearer had come the hour when there would be no dust atoms left and the whole hideous business would have reached a point of stability and therefore be beyond cure. He was becoming inwardly—and very frequently outwardly—frantic. So far there had been no response to his advertisement and he was loath to take the matter to official quarters for fear he would appear too ridiculous, or else some type of scientific plagiarist who could only be a genius if stimulated by the idea of another.

Not being aware of his thoughts and afraid of getting her head bitten off Elsie kept discreetly silent most of the time doing her now trivial housework, sewing, darning, and cooking, not daring to look into the abyss where no money was.

Definitely trouble and strife descended upon the dustless world in the passing weeks. The farmers in Britain and most of Europe rose in a body and made vehement protests to their respective governments. This was the spring of the year, the time of the rains and the snow—and there was nothing but the barren black skies and endless stars. Never any dew, never any frost. Rivers and brooks at their lowest ebb for many years and becoming gradually less as a state of absolute drought was declared throughout Britain and most of Europe.

Then the Blackness reached the shores of America and the hullabaloo which went up could have been heard in high heaven. What were the British scientists doing that they couldn't halt this deadly menace? The American physicists would soon get to work and put things right. Only it did not work out that way. The American scientists, like the British, failed ingloriously and the Darkness went on spreading. By the end' of February it had covered all the United States, producing aridity, intense coldness, immaculate cleanness, and panic.

The skin disease prevalent in Britain and Europe now also hit America, and with it a curious eye complaint caused, so the astronomers believed, by certain radiations of the sun, usually masked, affecting the eye's delicate cornea. The trouble was more noticeable in sunny and tropical climes, on which the Darkness was fast encroaching, and thousands found themselves suffering from defective vision.

The position had by now become desperate. In England, Timothy Brown had become almost forgotten, it being assumed that he had found the problem too much for him, and in any case the situation was far too serious now be entrusted to one man who had not even the recommendation of being a trained scientist.

The world's governments convened a conference to review the situation, an action brought about by public demand. But the meeting amounted to exactly nothing, except the consumption of foodstuffs, which could ill be spared. The scientists were at one in their statement that they could find no answer, so all humanity could do was make the best of things, One sensible action seemed to be to conscript labour from already crumbling business enterprises and turn it to account in the filtration of sea water. But this notion was quashed because, as one more prescient than the rest pointed out, there must soon come a time when the last drop of sea water would have been used up. And then what? Filtering sea water was only staving off the evil day.

The Blackness kept on spreading, until it was estimated that no more than two thousand miles of clear blue sky remained, and this was in the region of Central Africa where wind currents kept this one particular stretch remarkably free from dust even in the ordinary way, and therefore now presented something of a 'brake' on the disintegration.

The world was in a sorry mess. Approaching famine and present pestilence were rife. Plants, trees, and grass were shrivelled, not so much from the lack of water but because of the rays of the sun being so relentlessly unmasked. The one redeeming feature was that the atmosphere, as such, still existed, otherwise the blast of cosmic and solar radiation would long since have withered man from the face of the Earth.

And Timothy Brown? He had lost several pounds in weight and looked like a phantom, otherwise he was still on his feet and hoping that even yet he would find a way to reverse the awful thing he had brought about. He no longer stayed at home and slogged his memory, or worked on equations that usually turned out incorrect. Instead he roamed from morning until night, searching for some sign of that one boys' weekly he wanted. There was not a second-hand bookstall or magazine dealer in the whole of London that he did not visit. In the evenings he mapped out his 'round', and the next day carried it out—without success until the malignant fate that seemed bent on pursuing him at last relented on an evening in mid-March. It should have been a quiet, balmy time of year—but instead it was intensely cold, the only change in the season from winter being evidenced by the longer time the sun took to cut itself off neatly at the horizon.

Timothy was on his way home from a day's peregrinations when it happened. He had covered multitudes of brilliantly lighted streets, populated by downcast, hurrying people wrapped to the ears, when he saw a woman hurrying towards him with a carelessly wrapped package under her arm. She had passed in the intense glare before something registered in Timothy's mind. That front illustration on the paper round her package...

"Hey!" he yelled, swinging round. "Hey, madam! Miss! A moment, please!"

The woman, evidently not sure of whether Timothy was just another of the thugs who had become legion since the Blackness, accelerated her pace and broke into a run. Immediately Timothy did likewise, until he and the woman were tearing down street after street. At last, however, he overtook her, catching at her arm. Immediately she yanked herself free.

"Don't you dare touch me!" she shouted hoarsely, backing towards the wall.

"My dear lady, my apologies." Timothy was breathless as he raised his shabby hat. "I assure you I have a most urgent reason for my extraordinary behaviour."

"What reason?"

"That paper round the package you're carrying— Might I see it, please?"

Plainly astonished the woman unwrapped the periodical and handed it over. It was almost snatched from her. Like a prospector who has found gold Timothy searched the front page cartoon strip of Commander Rockjaw of the Space Patrol, and then opened the paper out quickly. His face fell.

"It's the right issue, August tenth last year," he said. "But where's the inside? This is only the first and last page. The cover, in fact."

"Look, what are you talking about?" the woman demanded.

"I want the rest of this paper. I'll pay any money, I'll go anywhere, but I must have the remainder."

"What are you, a crazy collector?"

"Yes," Timothy admitted, after a moment. "Where did you get that package? The paper came from there and I might find the rest of it."

The woman seemed to have decided by now that Timothy was not dangerous even though he was plainly a little queer.

"The paper didn't come from the shop, if you must know. They never wrap anything up in newsprint these days. It's from my own home. I don't know whether there's any more of it. I just snatched it up from Bobby's heap."

"Bobby's heap?" Timothy enquired, his eyes round and earnest.

"Bobby's my son, coming on fifteen. He reads this stuff and has dozens of back numbers pushed away on the dresser. I'd thought of clearing them out until dust started to vanish, then I thought it wasn't necessary."

"It's essential I get the centre of this paper," Timothy insisted. "Can I come with you?"

The woman shrugged, took back the useless part of the weekly, and returned it to her package. Without speaking she continued walking, and it was not long before they arrived it a moderately pleasant house.

"Wait!" the woman commanded, and went in and shut the door—Timothy waited, gazing at the sunlight opposite and shivering in the icy shadows that lay here. There was a deathly quiet on the metropolis and the stars were gleaming steel in the void overhead.

Then the woman returned and slightly opened the door on its chain. She thrust forth a grubby square of folded, printed paper.

"Here it is," she announced curtly. "Now go away."

"Madam, you will never know—" Timothy stopped as the door closed in his face. He quickly unfolded the paper but in the dark shadow he could not read it—so he began running to the nearest point where floodlighting was in operation. His hands trembled as he read the nearly threadbare pages, part of the printing obliterated on the crease.

"Eureka!" he whispered. "This is it—!"

When he entered his flat it was at the speed of a whirlwind and Elsie, reclining on the sofa, looked up with a start.

"I got it!" Timothy shouted, doing a war-dance. "I found what I wanted! Let this be a lesson to you never to burn or touch anything of mine again without asking me if you may."

Elsie got up, staring over her husband's shoulders.

"'…and then the great Professor Greycell had his great idea,'" Timothy muttered, reading aloud, "'He would throw into reverse the mighty machine which had shaken the world. He would reverse equation nine and there would lie the secret of how to—'" Timothy skipped several paragraphs and looked up. "It's it," he said briefly. "I can go to work again, and the faster the better with only two thousand miles of clear sky left."

So, his wanderings over, he plunged once more into computations, starting where he had left off on the fateful day when Elsie had burned his precious weekly. She relapsed into her habitual silence again and let him work on and on.

Not everybody was cursing the Blackness. That the astronomers were pleased with it has already been recorded but there were also others, chiefly the archaeologists. These mainly venerable gentlemen, oblivious to threatening conditions by reason of being so absorbed in their work, were discovering things about antiquity, which were breathtaking. And why? Because the death of dust was rendering crystal clear many priceless hieroglyphics and symbols belonging to ancient civilizations and adding a wealth of knowledge to the story of man's ascent from the troglodyte.

Meanwhile, Timothy Brown was still struggling with his ideas for an answer to the world's problems. And, with the ingenious way he had of transposing a vague theory into an actual fact, he had planned out something, which, to him at least, seemed reasonably certain of success. He promptly rang up Henderson.

"Who?" Henderson asked listlessly. "Brown? Brown?"

"Timothy Brown!" Timothy shouted, crouched in the call box. "You can't have forgotten me? If you have, take a look at the sky!"

"Oh yes, of course." Henderson became more alert. "Sorry Mr. Brown, I'm very much preoccupied these days. Well, what's the trouble?"

"Trouble? No trouble at all. I think I have the answer. It has taken a bit of doing but I've worked out a 'segregating screen' formula."

Henderson slowly got on his feet, the telephone glued to his ear.

"You've what?"

Timothy repeated his statement and added dolefully, "The thing that's troubling me is lack of finance. I can't afford to make a model from my plans. Any suggestions?"

"Definitely I have! Come over here immediately! Why on earth do you waste time telephoning?"

"I thought I'd better see first if I might still be welcome. Shan't be long."

Timothy rang off and for the next fifteen minutes Henderson waited impatiently, conjuring with the amazing possibility that perhaps Timothy had actually succeeded where everybody else had failed. At last he arrived, his bundles of notes, formulae, and everything else all wrapped in brown paper and carried as though it were salvage.

"That's it," he said, dumping the load on Henderson's desk.

"I see." Henderson opened the parcel and stared. "Er—where do we begin?"

"You don't have to read all the notes unless you wish to. That top sheet marked 'Final' is the sum total of everything. A sketch is attached to it so that a model can be built—I'm sure it ought to work."

"Well, we've tried everything else," Henderson sighed, "so what's one more? Pardon me—" He switched on the inter-phone. "Paget? Oh, will you step in my office a moment. Perhaps we have something."

Paget, the chief physicist, came in a moment or two later. He studied the notes, murmured something to himself, then took the whole pile back into the laboratory and got his colleagues to work. For over an hour Timothy lounged in a chair, waiting, and watching Henderson bobbing in and out, sometimes looking pleased, sometimes anxious. In the end both Henderson and the chief physicist were all smiles.

"There is every reason to believe, Mr. Brown, that your optimism is justified," Henderson announced, "If the theory works out as well in practice as it does in theory we have our answer. How did you come to think of it?"

Timothy shrugged. "Oh, just mathematics and a flair for originality. The vibration-energy from that instrument of mine should give a fan-shaped extension of vibration upwards to a hundred-mile limit. If we calculate the disruption vibration at one hundred and eighty atomic frequencies—and that is about what it is—it stands to reason that the frequency of my Segregator, working transversely to the disrupting energy, and having a frequency of well over two thousand, will block the path of the disrupting atoms by means of a superior load, and thereby what clear sky and atmosphere is left will be saved. On the other side of the screen the atoms will blast themselves to extinction and so the trouble will end."

Henderson and Paget glanced at each other. In those well-chosen sentences, carefully rehearsed, Timothy had put the whole thing in a large-sized nutshell.

"We'll do it," Henderson decided abruptly. "We'll get a model made right away and also a mobile power-plant Then we'll get on the move to Central Africa where there still remains a patch of sky on which to make a test."

"Right," Timothy agreed promptly. "How long will you be?"

"This time tomorrow. I promise you."

"I'll be here," Timothy replied, and wandered out of the office thoughtfully.

From that moment Henderson spared no effort. Engineers were summoned and told what to do, regardless of everything else. Experts went to work assembling the chassis of Timothy's machine; and in other quarters a mobile power plant, fully capable of feeding the instrument's needs, was constructed. Meanwhile, the exact portion of Central Africa, where the sky remained clear was ascertained and pinpointed.

By the time Timothy arrived the following day everything was ready and a freight plane loaded. He was greeted cordially and then escorted to the plane. His only companions were Henderson and Paget—excluding the crew, For this test only two men were needed, experts in their line.

"From all accounts," Henderson said, when the plane was on its way through the black sky, "the region we want extends straight across what used to be called the Belgian Congo, which is the approximate central point, and thereafter it extends for about a thousand miles west and east. I have made arrangements for us to operate the model from Banorka, in the central region. We have there an experimental research station for tropical investigation, and there is a runway and everything we need."

"Right," was all Timothy Brown said, chiefly because he was at the plane's window, studying the astonishing view below. Everything looked as though it were on the moon, the sunlight dappling the higher parts of the landscape with intense white and leaving the rest in intense darkness.

"I should imagine," Paget said, "that astronomers on other worlds must be getting grey hairs trying to imagine what has happened to this poor old planet of ours. Imagine how we'd be baffled if Mars suddenly changed its appearance in the same fashion."

Timothy turned from the window at last, his expression pensive. The view was too monotonous to be interesting for long.

Henderson looked at him sharply. "Anything wrong, Mr. Brown. You look worried."

"I'm only hoping everything will be all right," Timothy replied.

Henderson frowned. "I don't see that there can be a shadow of doubt, surely. You are completely confident—or were—and we have also summed everything up."

"Just equation twenty-six which worries me," Timothy confessed. "I'm not very clear on that, and neither was Professor Greycell."

He broke off. In the silence that followed, except for the roar of the plane engines, he could imagine exactly what was passing through Henderson and Paget's minds.

"Who," demanded Henderson at last, "Is Professor Greycell? Sounds like a comic character. I never heard of him."

"Just—just an invention of mine." Timothy smiled weakly.

"Professor Greycell," Paget said with deliberate coldness, "Is a crazy scientist who featured some time ago in a boys' paper. My own son used to rave about him and even I was tickled at some of his ideas. As a scientist I felt quite interested." He paused, weighing things up, and Timothy watched him anxiously.

"Where does a comic fiction character come into it?" Henderson demanded in bewilderment.

"He doesn't," Timothy replied hastily. "Just forget what I said. I'm pretty well mixed up."

While Henderson and Paget turned things over in their minds the plane droned onwards, arriving at Banorka towards half past two in the afternoon. During the last half hour of the journey they had flown from the dustless dark of the stricken area into one which at first had been deeply foggy, and finally had changed to white, with pale blue sky, a masked sun, no stars, and here and there a cloud. It was like transit to heaven.

Banorka, beyond the research post, was crowded to the limit with refugees, many of them living in pure jungle surroundings, but willing to do so rather than endure the unnatural conditions existing in the remainder of the world. Within the research post itself, however, everything was orderly and well-guarded, the permanent staff hardly aware of the conditions reigning beyond this torrid spot.

After a break for rest and refreshment preparations were made. Timothy's model was taken to the centre of the big testing field, and after it came the mobile power plant with its heavy generator. This in turn was started up by the power-unit within the research station, and everything was ready to begin.

"Now, what exactly do you propose to do, Mr. Brown?" Henderson enquired. "Since this region is normal we are hardly likely to observe an effect, are we?"

"It's normal exactly overhead, yes," Timothy admitted, "but towards the south-east there, low down on the horizon, there is a yellowness where the Dark is slowly encroaching. I propose to direct my vibration over there— it has a hundred mile radius remember—and we'll see what happens."

"In other words, if after careful checking, the yellow is found to come no nearer, it means success?" Paget asked.

"Correct!" Timothy switched on, and manoeuvred his instrument on its universal bearings. In no direction was he hampered for the jungle had been removed for some distance around the research station to make way for aircraft, and up in the sky there was, of course, unlimited freedom.

The recording dials on the Segregator showed quite clearly that it was operating perfectly, but beyond that nothing was apparent.

"Naturally," Timothy said, looking at the distant yellow, "we can't judge anything from here. A hover-plane would be the best thing. Let us examine the point where my vibration is operating. You will surely have detectors here which will show whether atomic action is taking place or not."

"Yes," Henderson agreed—turning towards the research building, "I think we can manage that."

CHAPTER 5

The wrong plan

Thirty minutes later a research station hover-plane had gained the area where Timothy announced that his vibration—still switched on—was working. The hover-plane came to a stop and the special instruments for detecting atomic disintegration came into operation. In absorbed silence Henderson and Paget studied them, Timothy watching between them.

"That there is atomic disintegration in tremendous measure is more than obvious," Paget commented presently. "See those flares of energy across the screen? There we have it."

"Turn the detector slowly," Timothy instructed. "You should at length reach a point where there is a clearly defined line beyond which the disintegration is not operating. That line will be where my vibration is doing its segregating work."

Paget did as instructed, the pilot keeping the hover-plane reasonably steady in the process, but no matter how much Paget wangled and twisted the instrument, there was no dividing line. For twenty minutes he tried and met with complete failure.

"There must be a line!" Timothy insisted urgently. "It just couldn't be that—"

He paused, looking up anxiously. Paget and Henderson; noticed it at the same time. The glow of bright daylight through the windows was dying and paling to fog. Within a matter of seconds the fog was at maximum density; then it slowly cleared again and outside was a sky as black as Erebus with the stars glittering coldly amidst the sunshine.

"Standish!" Henderson barked to the pilot, who was surveying the phenomenon in bewilderment.

"Yes, Mr. Henderson?"

"Has this plane drifted or moved at all? Are we still at the point where we stopped?"

The pilot checked his instruments. "We haven't moved, sir."

Henderson turned to Timothy. "Well, Mr. Brown, what is the answer? Since we haven't moved it can only mean; that the area of disintegration has, and in so doing it has enveloped us. That means your Segregator isn't working! Or at least it isn't having an effect."

"It certainly looks that way," Timothy admitted, frowning. "I just don't understand it."

"If anything," Henderson commented, "the effect seems to have been accelerated. Formerly this area was quite free, and the encroachment was extremely slow. Now it seems to have speeded up. Something, some-where, is terribly wrong."

"Better get back to my Segregator and check it over," Timothy said. "Probably a fault somewhere. Remember, I have not even been allowed to have a look at its insides."

"Why should you need to?" Henderson demanded angrily. "Can't you trust the engineers to build from your plans?"

"Certainly, but the best of us make mistakes. Let's get back."

No further time was wasted and the hover-plane rapidly crossed the boundary line between disintegration and normalcy, finally alighting again at the research field. Instantly Timothy wrenched open the cabin door and hurried over to his instrument, switching it off.

"Where can I examine this thing?" he asked.

"Plenty of room in the laboratory," Henderson told him sourly. "This way—"

He led the way into the research building. Here, with the two scientists watching in stony calm, Timothy unscrewed the casing from his apparatus and peered at the insides in the bright light.

"Definitely something wrong," he said presently. "I never gave a wiring like this one."

"The engineers wouldn't put in something of their own fancy!" Henderson barked.

"I know. The winding is mine, but it's not the one I suggested in my plan—" Timothy straightened up and looked blank. "Good Lord!" he exclaimed.

"Well?" asked Paget icily. "Something occurred to you?"

"Yes. This isn't the Segregator. It's a crude design of the original dust destroyer. Both the destroyer and the segregator are alike in appearance, outwardly, which is why I did not suspect anything—"

"What the blue hell are you raving about?" Henderson exploded. "How can this be a crude design of the original destroyer? The plans and sketches you gave us—"

"Which did you check?" Timothy interrupted. "When you spent so long going through the notes?"

"We checked the computations and maths concerning the vibration of the Segregator," Paget replied. "And they were quite in order. Theoretically, I could have sworn you had something."

"But the sketch and plans for the model. Did you check those?"

"There seemed no need with time so precious. We assumed that must be right."

"That's where the mistake has come in," Timothy groaned, smiting his forehead. "The engineers wouldn't concern themselves with the computations: they'd build the model exactly from the plan—and I provided the wrong one."

"You—what?" Henderson's calmness was frightening.

"Just—just a mistake," Timothy said uneasily. "I have so many plans and sketches, I must have given you the wrong one. I thought I'd discarded this one long ago when I made my improved dust destroyer. All we did just now was accelerate the dust destruction for a while. Now we've switched off the Blackness will spread at the same slow rate as before—"

"Then where is the plan we want?" Paget snapped.

"I suppose it must be at home, probably with my early notes. In my excitement I must have picked up the wrong one."

Silence. Timothy looked from one man to the other. "It's that confounded equation twenty-six," he sighed. "It appears in both cases which explains my natural mistake."

"Nothing can explain a mistake like this!" Henderson barked. "We have wasted hours of valuable time, made endless preparations, all to be told you have provided the wrong plan! Putting it plainly, Mr. Brown, you are a damned fool!"

"I admit it. However, I can return home for the right plan and then you can—"

"We are not interested," Henderson interrupted. "Do you think for one moment I would trust any longer to your insane notions? I had difficulty enough getting the engineers to build your projector as it was: I'd certainly never manage it a second time."

"But surely—"

"No!" Henderson stated flatly. "A plane will be provided to take you home. And think yourself lucky that legal proceedings are not being taken against you! At any normal time they would be!"

There was nothing more Timothy could do. He was completely in the dog-house. An hour later he was seated morosely in a London-bound plane, his bundles of notes in brown paper on his knees. He was the only passenger. Though Henderson and Paget were also returning to London they evidently preferred to do it by themselves.

"The whole thing's such a pity," Timothy told his wife, when at last he arrived home again. "I'm sure I've got the whole thing worked out, yet I haven't got the money to build the apparatus—and from here on Henderson just won't look at me."

"Your own fault for being so silly," Elsie stated frankly. "Here, have some stew. Maybe you'll feel better."

Timothy lost himself in thought and ate absently. Then when the meal was over he spent an hour searching through the incredible piles of papers, which constituted the notes of his research. It was pretty near to midnight when at last he found what he was seeking.

"Here it is!" He waved a sketch in the air triumphantly. "I was beginning to think that perhaps I'd destroyed it."

His mood changed. "Not that it signifies anything. Even though I have found it it's just a useless piece of paper."

"Oh no it isn't!" Elsie declared. "You said yourself that if these conditions are not altered it means the end of the world. You don't imagine I'm going to let you sit around with the key to victory and have you do nothing about it, do you?"

"But what can I do? Henderson's the big noise and I've already told you how he feels. He'll never give me a hearing again."

"He must be made to somehow. One man with his silly ideas can't be allowed to stand in the way of humanity's salvation."

Elsie looked surprised at her own statement and wondered for a moment whether it were not perhaps worthy of handing down to posterity.

"Only alternative is to try the Government," Timothy roused. "Won't be easy since Henderson will doubtless advertise it far and wide that I am not to be trusted. Oh, I don't know. I'll sleep on it and then decide in the morning."

During the night endless numbers of factories which had been working exclusively on the installation intended to handle Timothy Brown's hoped-for 'Segregator'—so that many areas at once could be handled—received order to dismantle all equipment and turn over to other work. Timothy Brown was a failure. So, between the devil and deep blue sea, Henderson also retired grimly to bed.

The clear sky over Central Africa narrowed imperceptibly, until at last there must come a time when only one round spot remained. When that went the light would also go out for all civilization.

The next day Timothy's mind was made up. He would visit the prime minister, or if that failed then the highest authority he could contact. Convinced of his Segregator, and in possession of the right plan he set out for Downing Street. But Downing Street was not interested in Timothy, chiefly because he was little known and his part in the dust destroying business was hardly known beyond a select circle of scientists with Henderson at their head.

At the end of the day Timothy was no nearer. He seemed to have walked miles through the dustless streets and blinding sunlight, or cooled off rapidly in the Stygian shadows. Once he even thought of trying Henderson again, but the remembrance of his bitter, uncompromising expression changed his mind.

He returned home, so utterly beaten by failure that even Elsie had not the heart to chide him. She fed him and made him some tea, then relapsed into dead silence until some new turn of thought should possess him.

And in the outside world the authorities had their hands full trying to forestall panic. Unless the dust crisis was averted, it would not be long before rioting and looting, murder and arson, began.

At home Timothy Brown was also stuck. He sat on the sofa, peering into the smokeless fire, listening to the latest radio reports. Elsie listened too, darning a sock meanwhile.

"...the latest report from the Metropolitan Water Board shows that the water supply for London is dropping at an accelerated speed. From today it will become a punishable offence to use water for any purpose except drinking and essential washing. During the hours of ten in the morning to six in the evening all water will be cut off."

"Huh!" Elsie commented in disgust. "How am I supposed to prepare meals?"

"…The state of drought prevalent in the United States is in no wise altered and in many areas cattle are now dying in their hundreds. It was stated in Congress today that if something is not done quickly to foster better relations with more fortunate countries, which so far have not been fully enveloped by the Darkness, there—"

"Oh, damn!" Timothy swore, and switched off. "All this confounded yelling from all sides and here am I, hamstrung for a few miserable pounds to build a test projector. If things were not so upset and most businesses in ruins I'd contact a moneylender and pay him off when I'd justified myself to Henderson."

Elsie did not answer. She was staring straight in front of her, her darning needle half raised. She looked as though she expected an earthquake any moment.

"I said—" Timothy began, with laboured calm, then Elsie interrupted him explosively.

"Foster!"

"Eh? What do you mean—Foster?"

"He said a moment ago something about 'to foster better relations'. It started me thinking. What about Foster? The one you tried to sell your cleaner to in the first place?"

"What about him?" Timothy asked gloomily. "He very soon slammed the door in my face when he saw what my dust destroyer could do."

"I know, but if this Segregator is all you say it is he might be willing to take a chance on a model of it. Think what it would mean to him and his firm—and to us—if the Segregator worked and the Kleen Sweep Brush Company saved all civilization!"

Timothy's eyes opened wider. "I never thought of that!"

"I know you didn't: I did. Better ring up Foster right away—or better still go and see him and take your plan with you."

"No use at this hour. His offices will be shut—even granting his business is still in existence, which I shouldn't think it will be— Where's the directory?"

Timothy yanked it from amidst his few books. It was very much dated, but it might still serve its purpose. He ran his finger down the Fosters and gave a grunt.

"About a dozen Jacob Fosters in private residence. Might be any of them. I'll go along to his offices and see what I can find out."

"Take your plan and equations with you. Once catch that big bag of wind in the right mood and the thing's done. You might not get a second chance."

Timothy plunged out into the rarefied coldness of the spring night. He knew his way easily enough from his earlier trip, though he did not particularly enjoy the journey he made. There were bands of men and women roaming the blackened streets, some of them quite harmless and merely singing amongst themselves to keep up their spirits—but others were obviously of the hooligan, type, taking every advantage of the abnormal conditions to break the law.

He could not help but notice the decline that had struck this great city since the coming of the Blackness. Though the streets were spotless and ordinary litter was still removed daily, there was a deathly look about everything. Many buildings were shuttered, others had broken windows, men and women lounged at the corners of the streets.

Here and there a religious fanatic yelled and shouted that the wrath of God was come upon His people. There was no longer any normalcy in things. Most of the places of entertainment were shut; many streets were without lighting entirely as water shortage demanded slowing down of subsidiary powerhouse generators. There was the definite stamp of decay and doom in the air.

Shaken considerably by the realization of what his own meddling had brought about Timothy finally arrived at the Kleen Sweep Brush Company. Across the main door, visible in the one light further up the street, was placarded one word—CLOSED. Icy wind was whipping papers past the boarded doors and whistling through the windows smashed by hooligan elements.

Once again Timothy was up a gum tree. He turned away disconsolately and glanced further up the street. His eye wandered to the lights of a still thriving café almost opposite the former Kleen Sweep Brush Company. There existed the slim possibility that the great Foster perhaps went in there now and again for a snack; so Timothy entered the nearly deserted place, glanced around him on the spotless, entirely normal surroundings, and decided it was not a bad bet. Foster would perhaps have graced a place like this with his presence.

Timothy found it easy to gain attention since no customers were in the place at the moment. The proprietor, evidently working on 'business as usual' lines, came into view in resplendent evening dress, clearly not deeply enamoured of the shabby little man with the seedy overcoat and floppy trilby.

"Sorry to bother you," Timothy apologized, "but do you know—or did you once know—a man called Jacob Foster?"

"Supposing I did? Nothing wrong in it." The proprietor seemed to get the impression Timothy was stooging for the police and his eyes became uncompromising.

"I'm an old friend of his," Timothy explained. "I didn't know he'd closed his business and, things being so upset, I am wondering how to get in touch with him. Think you can help me?"

The proprietor, realizing he was not involved, thawed a little. "You mean a big, hefty chap with wild hair?"

"That's Foster!"

"Yes, he came in here every day for his lunch. Let's see—he lives, or did do, out Hampstead way. Can't tell you where."

"That narrows the circle a little anyhow," Timothy said. "Maybe I could trace him in the phone directory, if you happen to have one?" The proprietor motioned to the three directories on the telephone table and Timothy went across to them. "I'll have a cup of tea and a sandwich," he added, feeling he ought to do something besides ask questions. They were provided, the proprietor doing all his own serving, and Timothy ploughed steadily through the eighteen odd Jacob Fosters in the Hampstead area. Finally he put down money he could ill afford. "To cover the phone calls I want to make," he explained. "If you have no objection."

"Go ahead," the proprietor agreed, somewhat coldly—so for nearly an hour Timothy rang up each Jacob Foster in turn and got the wrong one. In most cases there was no answer at all. He had reached the penultimate chance when the voice in the receiver nearly deafened him.

"Well, well, what is it? Jacob Foster speaking!"

"Formerly of the Kleen Sweep?" Timothy cried excitedly.

"Certainly! Who else? What can I do for you?"

"This is Timothy Brown speaking, Mr. Foster. You remember me, surely?"

"Remember you! Good heavens, how could I ever forget you? Wherever I look there is evidence of you and your crazy dust destroyer!"

Timothy glanced around him, but the café was still empty. The proprietor, however, was just beyond the screen and hearing every word. His expression changed surprisingly as he heard Timothy identify himself; then he slipped quickly in the back regions, presently returning and looking quite unconcerned. In the course of his perambulating around the café, however, he gently slipped the bolt over the door.

"All I want to do is see you, sir," Timothy insisted. "It's vitally important and I know I can interest you. I can't explain it over the phone. Just grant me a few words—please."

There was silence at the other end of the line.

"This can probably save the world!" Timothy added urgently.

"Mmmm... I only wish I was not so biased against you, Mr. Brown. However— Very well, come and see me. I'll expect you within the next half hour."

"Right!" Timothy put down the phone eagerly and headed for the café door, glancing at the proprietor as he went. "Thanks for the help. I managed to contact him."

"Good," the proprietor responded sourly.

Timothy reached the door and pulled uselessly at the handle. He rattled it and tugged, then looked at the proprietor again. He had come round the small counter now, grim menace in his face. Timothy hesitated, desperately uncertain.

"The—the door's stuck," he explained.

"For your edification, Mr. Brown, the door is locked, and it's staying that way! Half the population of London want to have a few words with you—and not pleasant words either."

"I can't stop now; I'm in a hurry!" Again Timothy wrenched at the door. Then he added with sudden authority. "Get this door open! How dare you detain me against my will?"

"Don't be funny! Sit down on that chair."

Timothy looked at the chair indicated, one of those beside the nearest table, and at length he did as he was told. Then he looked up sharply at a sudden commotion from the kitchen regions of the café. There were angry voices, the sound of many feet, and presently about a score or so of men and women came into view, slowing down as they saw Timothy staring at them in plain fright.

"A small representative party of the hundreds who are after your blood, Mr. Brown," the proprietor explained. "I thought I recognized you when you came in here. When you identified yourself over the telephone that settled everything—"

"What on earth are you talking about?" Timothy broke in hotly. "Let me out of here! I'll have the police on you for this."

"You know perfectly well that the police are otherwise occupied, and any case you're not leaving here just yet. It is even possible that you may not be aware of the fact when you do leave here! As for what this is all about: take a look!"

Timothy found an evening newspaper flung at him. It was only a single sheet, as were most newspapers at this present critical time—but the information contained on that single sheet was devastating.

SCIENTIFIC CHIEF NAMES
CREATOR OF DARKNESS

In a special statement to the press today, Mr. Roy Henderson, chief of the Scotland Yard scientific division, who has recently been engaged with other scientists in an effort to restore normal conditions to our stricken world, named one man as the cause of the present desperate crisis. He stated that though this man, Timothy Brown, a former solicitor's clerk, could not legally be accused for the tragic scientific blunder which destroyed dust on our planet, it in no way absolves him from blame. This man…

The statement rambled on and on, through three; columns, but Timothy was feeling too sick to read it. He saw his own photograph staring up at him and wondered how it had been obtained. From the background it was apparently a press photo taken at the time when Timothy had embarked for Central Africa aboard the special plane.

"Well?" demanded the café proprietor bitterly. "Satisfied?"

"You shouldn't believe all you read in the newspapers," Timothy replied uncomfortably. "Mr. Henderson is an enemy of mine and he is deliberately trying to get me into trouble. In any case you heard me say just now over the telephone that I have an invention which can save us all. Mr. Foster can very soon—"

"We're not interested in Foster—only you. People have been wondering for long enough if some crackpot were at the root of our troubles, and now we have the facts. It is the people who have suffered, therefore it is for them to say what should be done to you."

"Now look here—!" Timothy sprang to his feet, but whatever further words he had intended were smothered as he was seized in the rough hands of the mob and borne, struggling helplessly, through the café's rear regions into the yard.

For Timothy the minutes which followed were a blurred confusion. He was carried along by the men and women as they shouted at the top of their voices, and from the streets leading off the big main one more men and women came, most of them of the hooligan element. They were told quickly who the victim was in the midst, and so the word vas passed on. By the time Timothy had been brought to an old deserted section of land where a big building had once stood, there must have been many hundreds of angry men and women in the glow of the distant street lamps.

"Burn him!" yelled somebody.

"That's right, burn him! Same as the Plague does to your skin! Give him a taste of his own medicine."

"Strip him and throw cold water on him. He'll freeze solid in a few minutes'."

Many and varied were the ghoulish suggestions for disposing of Timothy Brown, to none of which he raised any protest since he was too utterly scared. But amongst the crowd there was still the café proprietor, saner than the rest, and it was he who kept things in focus.

"Law, as such, is pretty well dead," he said. "The people have no respect for it any more, so they've formulated laws of their own. You, Brown, are about the most hated man in London, if not in the world. You've brought more tragedy upon human beings than all the warlords who ever existed, but for all that you are entitled to a trial and the chance to defend your actions. We'll have that trial this moment— Anybody here who wishes to speak in Brown's defence?"

The only response was angry shouts, at which Timothy shook himself free of the hands holding him.

"I'll do my own defending," he retorted. "You know who I am and what I am reputed to have done. Dust has gone, the skies are black—save for one precious area over Africa—and all the civilization of the world has been disorganized. Do you think I'm the kind of man who'd bring such a state of affairs about willingly?"

"Frankly, no," admitted the café proprietor. "You look a henpecked little devil to me."

"I'm a quiet, middle-class man with a liking for things scientific," Timothy stated. "I invented a device to help the housewife through her drudgery, something went wrong, and chain reaction of dust atoms set in. I'm not going into all the wearying details because you know as well as I do what has happened since. But I will say this: I have the solution to it all in my pocket at this moment, the plan of a projector to reverse the trouble that has been caused. And what happens? Nobody in high circles will listen to me. Henderson thinks I'm a lunatic. My last bet is Jacob Foster, to whom I went in the first instance. That's my story. Let me go free and see Foster and within a week, or less, things will start returning to normal."

"It's a get-out!" shouted a woman on the fringe of the crowd. "Once he goes free we'll never see him again. Finish him off while we have the chance."

"Where is that plan, did you say?" the proprietor asked.

"In my pocket, and it's stopping there!"

In this Timothy was more sanguine than discreet. Before he realized what had happened his pockets had been emptied and he was lying on the ground with his old overcoat in shreds. By this time the situation had grown ugly, and the café proprietor had lost his grip on the mob.

"We'll use this bit of paper to start off the bonfire!" shouted the man who had rifled Timothy's pockets. "Gather some wood and we'll finish this ourselves."

Bewildered, his face bleeding from a blow on the cheek, Timothy floundered to his feet. Dully he stood watching the people surging hither and yon in the gloom, searching for wood wherewith to erect his funeral pyre. Nearby the man who had stolen the precious plan was waving it in the air.

Then Timothy suddenly realized how desperate was his position. Everything, including his life, would be lost if he didn't act instantly. For about the first and only time in his life he lashed out his right fist with every vestige of his strength. It struck the man with the plan behind the ear, and since he was not expecting it he reeled sideways and stumbled. In those split seconds Timothy lunged in a flying tackle, grabbed the man round the knees, and brought him on his face to the ground.

The people were too scattered by now to realize what was happening—and Timothy knew it. He stooped, snatched the precious plan from the sprawling man's fingers, and then began to run. He tripped, stumbled, collided with old building foundations, but kept going—and the exceptional density of the darkness beyond the range of the scattered street lights was his salvation. He gained a crumbled alcove where a doorway had once stood and remained there, recovering his breath and shaking with reaction. All around him were shouts and the noise of feet. The only thing visible was a segment of distant roof, black against the utter starry dark. Down here no light penetrated. The diffusion, even of the night, which had once existed, was no more.

At length the sounds began to abate and there was silence. Cautiously, moving only foot by foot, Timothy began to emerge from his hiding place. He crept over debris and bricks, all of them quite dustless, and at length, by a circuitous route, succeeded in gaining the main road about a mile from the scene of his alarming experiences. Here he looked up and down anxiously for some sign of a taxi. There were still taxis plying for hire in spite of the conditions, but on this occasion there was none in sight. Only a powerful car approaching from the city.

Timothy grunted to himself and began walking along slowly, ready to run for it if more danger showed. He pondered the idea of thumbing a lift from the approaching car and glanced over his shoulder towards it. He prepared to bolt as it started to slow down. More trouble evidently—!

"Hey there! Mr. Brown! Come back here!"

Timothy slowed down in his run as he recognized the voice. There could only be one voice like that anywhere. Slowly he returned and peered cautiously at the face framed in the open rear window.

"So it is you, Mr. Foster!"

"Certainly it is." Foster boomed. "Get in! This is a lucky stroke if ever there was one. I thought I'd lost you."

Timothy floundered into the car and sank into the cushions. Foster gave a brief word to his chauffeur and the car started up again, speeding through the ill-lighted gloom.

"This is the queerest coincidence ever," Timothy said at last. "How in the world did you find me?"

"All perfectly simple, Mr. Brown. When you didn't turn up at my home after half an hour had gone I began to think something must have happened to you: I'm perfectly aware of the hooligan element reigning at the present time, believe me. So I traced the spot from where you had phoned by means of the telephone exchange and drove over. First thing I saw was a mob of people shouting to each other that you'd vanished. I stood about and gathered enough to realize that you'd escaped something pretty nasty. I hoped you might show up again. When you didn't I gave it up and started for home—and saw you ahead."

"I'm surprised you went to the trouble of looking for me. From the way you sounded over the phone I gathered that you weren't particularly anxious to give me a hearing."

"I wasn't," Foster replied, his voice overpowering in the small confines of the car. "But then I got to thinking about your final words, something about saving the world. That appealed to me immensely. I couldn't possibly let you slip—I only hope that this idea is not as crazy as your last one."

"It's the genuine thing," Timothy declared.

"I believe you. And do you know why? Because no man, however crazy, would stick up for his beliefs as strongly as you appear to have done against the mob, if he didn't have infinite faith in himself. That experience has done a lot to make me consider you favourably. Mr. Brown— Is that the plan in your hand there?"

Timothy nodded and unfurled the crumpled remains. It was still the plan, though severely creased.

"We'll soon straighten it out," Foster said. "And what exactly is your proposition? Why come to me when the government ought to know?"

Timothy skated around the fact that the Government—and Henderson—were sick of him, and replied:

"I felt I owed it to you to have the first chance since I began my business with you and then ruined things. My trouble is capital. I've hardly a bean."

"I see. Believe me I haven't much myself either since my firm closed up—thanks to you."

"I can put it back on its feet again, and your firm can become known as the one which saved humanity. You can put all this horror right by bringing dust back instead of removing it, as you used to."

"And that is the plan with which to accomplish it?"

"It is. Build a model of this projector, fly me to Central Africa before the last strip of blue sky vanishes, and I'll show you a miracle. You can take the entire credit. All I want is to put things right."

"We'll discuss this fully at my home." Foster decided, and he gave the chauffeur orders to accelerate.

CHAPTER 6

The final gamble

Once Foster's home was reached no time was wasted. Foster led the way to the library, had the manservant bring in refreshment in the shape of sandwiches and coffee, and then the analysis of Timothy's much battered plan began. The more he listened the more baffled Foster plainly became.

"I see the idea about a curtain of vibration cutting off the good from the bad areas," he said at last, "but as far as the scientific issues go I'm utterly lost. I've told you before. I'm a commercial man, not a scientist."

"Can't you take my word for it?" Timothy demanded.

"I suppose so," Foster was somewhat begrudging. "The trouble is I haven't yet forgotten the mess that dust destroyer of yours brought about—all through taking your word. If the same thing happened again—"

"It couldn't possibly. Put up the money to have a model built from this plan and I'll very soon show you."

Foster reflected for a moment or two and then finally nodded.

"All right! Let it never be said that Jacob Foster is afraid to take a chance—I'll contact the manufacturers who used to turn out my vacuum cleaners. They'll give priority to anything I want."

"Sooner the better," Timothy said anxiously. "Every moment counts. I've got to work on that spot of blue sky over Central Africa before it entirely disappears—granting it hasn't gone already."

Foster reached for the telephone. "I'll get busy this very moment. "I can get Wilson, the managing director of the engineers at his home, I think."

Foster guessed right and in a moment or two Wilson was on the line.

"New type of projector?" he repeated. "Yes. "I suppose we can manage it, Jacob, but what sort of a thing is it? Anything complicated about it?"

Foster put his hand over the mouthpiece and turned to Timothy.

"Would you say your plan is complicated?"

"Only in the matter of windings, but there's nothing a good engineer can't do."

Foster nodded and resumed telephoning, handing the information on.

"That's just the trouble," Wilson said. "The windings will need copper wire and I can't get that these days without a Government permit."

"What!" Foster exploded. "Since when have—"

"In case you missed it," Wilson interrupted dryly, "there is a crisis, and it's rumoured that all over the world Governments are building spaceships, our own included. Maybe the high-ups are trying to save themselves—though God knows how fleeing into space would help them… Whatever the real reasons for it, a licence has now to be obtained for all metal, wire, and other basic requirements of an engineering job. Easy enough: just advise the Government of your wishes, state what it is for, and you'll get your licence quickly enough."

"I'll ring you back," Foster said, and put the phone down. Timothy could tell from the big man's expression that something was radically wrong.

"There's only one way out of this," Foster said at last. "You'll have to build the projector model yourself. I'll put up the money if you can get the materials."

"But—why?" Timothy stared blankly.

Foster gave him the reason and then added, "You'll never get a licence in a hundred years, or will you? Since it has been in all the papers that you started the present disaster I can hardly see you being granted permission to meddle further— Not that I think you're meddling, but you know what a Government official would think."

Timothy groaned. "That's only part of the opposition against me, Mr. Foster—" and he related what had happened when he had tried to demonstrate before Henderson.

"So that's it!" Foster exclaimed finally. "You were not really anxious to give me the first chance; you tried me because nobody else would have you!"

"Yes, but—" Timothy hesitated. "I still stick to it that I have the solution."

"And I believe you because of the way you refuse to be shaken!" Foster's expression suddenly cleared. "I haven't forgotten you stood up for your rights before the mob, you know. Mmmm, this is difficult. A licence is right out, and getting the necessary requirements by undercover means would be dangerous at a time like this. If I could—and there's no guarantee of it—could you make the required model?"

"I could, yes, but with none of the necessary machinery to speed things up I might be too late. It would perhaps take me several weeks to complete the job. That is, unless I—"

Timothy stopped, his eyes brightening with a sudden thought. Foster watched him intently.

"Basically," Timothy hurried on, "this Segregator has the same design as the original dust destroyer: the difference lies in the internal windings. Now, back at the laboratory. Henderson still has my original dust destroyer. If I could get hold of that—and I can't think why I shouldn't since it is my own property—I could very soon convert it. Matter of a few hours. The only drawback is I told Henderson he could do what he liked with it as I didn't want it any longer!"

"You're crazier than I thought. Mr. Brown." Foster declared. "However it's our only chance so we've got to take it. Better get in touch with Henderson right away. There's nothing I can do for you since that instrument belongs to you. Here's the telephone. Get busy."

Timothy nodded. He was feeling immensely bolstered with Jacob Foster's powerful personality supporting him. So he rang the Physical Research Laboratory and was informed Henderson had gone home. The second time round Henderson answered.

"Yes? Henderson here—"

"Timothy Brown speaking, Dr. Henderson. I would—"

"What!" Henderson's voice was so loud it could be clearly heard by Foster. "Didn't I tell you never to contact me again? What the devil do you mean by taking up my time like this? Can't you—"

"I'd like my dust destroyer back." Timothy put in quietly.

"Oh, you would, would you? Well, you're not getting it! You told me to keep it, and you said that in front of witnesses in the laboratory—"

"I don't care what I said. I still want it. Not in pieces, as it was at the time of your analysis, but exactly in the form I gave it to you when I was ordered to hand it over."

"Now you listen to me. Mr. Brown—"

"No, you listen!" Foster interrupted, taking the phone from Timothy's indecisive grasp. "Get that dust destroyer properly built up again. Dr. Henderson, and have it ready for collection by nine tomorrow morning. You've no legal authority for retaining it. That you are the chief scientist for the Yard's scientific division doesn't make any difference to the rights of Mr. Brown, Understand?"

"Who am I talking to now?" Henderson demanded.

"Jacob Foster of the former Kleen Sweep Brush Company—and you will not do as you like with me, sir. Indeed, if you were not so short-sighted and wrapped up in red tape you could save civilization this minute, through the agency of Mr. Brown. Since you have thrown away that chance—"

"Thrown it away!" Henderson sounded as though somebody were strangling him. "Thrown it away! Didn't that nincompoop of a Brown tell you what he did? Gave me the wrong plan! Had us playing around in Central Africa."

"I know all about that and any man, particularly one with so much scientific detail on his mind, is liable to make a mistake. You had no right to debar Mr. Brown because of one slip like that. It's out of your hands now in any case. When things are back to normal, as they very soon will be, you are going to look the biggest fool in Britain—if not the world! I'll see to that."

"Now look here. Mr. Foster—"

"Have that apparatus ready for nine." Foster snapped, and rang off.

Timothy rubbed his hands. "That was magnificent, Mr. Foster."

"He's a bigot," Foster growled. "I only hope this darned thing of yours works after all that or the laugh will be on me. I'm taking a second—and a terrible—chance on you. Mr. Brown."

Timothy smiled. "It'll be all right. All I need now is copper wire, about five hundred feet of it, so I can make the necessary new windings the moment I go to work tomorrow."

"I'll see what I can do," Foster promised. "Now you'd better be getting back home. I'll have you driven there so no mobs can get at you. Call at the Physical Laboratory tomorrow morning—I'll send the car over for you—and get your apparatus. If Henderson has not had it made ready for you report to me and I'll very soon fix it. I'm friendly with Government authorities who can very soon put him in his place."

"Then couldn't yon talk them into giving me a proper hearing?"

"I could, but I won't. Your faith in this Segregator has been transmitted to me too and I want to be in on this great moment when you stop the Blackness spreading."

So Timothy departed and was duly driven home. His serene smile upon arrival made Elsie regard him hopefully, and over a cup of tea he explained everything that had happened.

"Good job I thought of Foster!" she exclaimed. "He's a windbag, of course, but he'll probably see the thing through."

"Definitely he will—chiefly for what he can get out of it."

Timothy fell into worried thought and Elsie looked at him anxiously.

"Nothing wrong, is there? You're not getting the feeling that perhaps you might not be able to manage it after all?"

"Good heavens, no! I've no fears whatever on that score. I'm just wondering if it is possible to slightly alter the original windings on the dust destroyer so that it really does destroy dust without starting chain reaction. It's an idea, you know," Timothy went on eagerly. "In the course of going through my various formulae I've worked out, in my mind that is, a way of compromising."

"Compromising?" Elsie was looking vacant again. "With what?"

"With the original wavelength that started the chain reaction. You see, the vibration that forms the segregating curtain is at the opposite end of the vibratory scale, which began the chain reaction, therefore at somewhere mid-way there must exist just exactly the right vibration for destroying dust atoms without sufficient power to start them off into a chain reaction. Remember our chorus girl simile where I described the first one falling over and knocking down the whole row? Well, in this instance the first chorus girl would only lurch, without sufficient strength to knock over her neighbour, though she herself would fall. It's like that. Or am I too technical?"

"Much," Elsie replied. "All I have got to say is: take care what you're doing, Timothy Brown! If by some miracle you do succeed in curing our trouble, don't for the love of heaven start it all off again to try out some new theory. There won't be any escape next time—"

"Or a marriage between segregating vibration and dust-atom vibration," Timothy mused, hardly hearing. "Yes, that might be it! If things go too far just switch on the twin segregator and the effect will be limited to that radius! I do believe—I have it!" he finished triumphantly. "The two wavelengths must work together. Then it's as safe as houses! Now don't talk to me while I work it out!"

Precisely what he had in mind Elsie did not ask, not because she was not interested but because she knew her limitations. So she let Timothy be, and at midnight he was still sprawled on the shabby old sofa, scribbling notes, working out equations, and tracing incomprehensible sketches of which Elsie had an occasional glimpse.

The next day there was a satisfied look about Timothy, the expression of a man who has achieved an ideal. Not that he said anything about it. He had an early breakfast, kissed Elsie goodbye, and then put on his hat and coat at exactly the moment the flat bell rang under the pressure of Foster's chauffeur's thumb.

Surprisingly—to Timothy at least, Henderson had obeyed Foster's instructions and the dust destroyer was ready, its outer casing in exactly the normal position. How the insides were had yet to the discovered. Timothy took the instrument from the caretaker, thankful that none of the scientific staff were on view to accost him, and departed again for Foster's home.

Foster was shaved, immaculate, and ready for action. He conducted Timothy into a spare room of the house, which had been roughly fitted up as a workshop with a powerful light trained over the main bench.

"There's the wire you asked for," Foster said, indicating a huge bobbin with the gleam of copper forming its centre. "It was difficult to get, but I managed it. Isn't much gets Jacob Foster down, believe me. Glad to see that fool of a Henderson did as he was told."

"Uh-huh," Timothy acknowledged, his mind on his job as he unfastened the base of his dust destroyer. When he came to examine the interior workings he gave a sigh of relief.

"Okay?" Foster asked anxiously.

"Yes, thank heaven. I'd had the fear that perhaps something might not have been put back properly, but I was wrong. Now I have to add the necessary wiring here."

"I see. And take the other one away?"

"That was my original idea, but since then I've hit on a much better notion. By welding the original coils—which caused all the trouble—to this new coiling it should be possible to produce a genuine dust destroyer, as well as a segregator which stops the effect spreading into chain reaction."

Foster looked uneasy. "All sounds very simple in theory. Mr. Brown, but don't you think it would be wiser to concentrate at the moment on the segregator, and nothing else?"

"I'm thinking of the future," Timothy replied. "You have to have a product worthy of selling, and this is about the only time I can make a genuine test. So I'm risking it."

Foster shrugged, reflected that matters could hardly become any worse now no matter what happened, and stood aside to watch Timothy at work. As he fixed the wiring in the position he required he asked a question.

"What's the latest news? I haven't heard anything since seven o'clock, and at that time blue sky was still in existence over Central Africa, but only in very narrow formation. A few more hours may see its extinction. This business for me, has developed into a race against time."

"I'll see what the latest news is," Foster replied, and left the room.

Shortly afterwards he returned, his expression troubled.

"Sands are running out," he said gravely, "The blue gap is down to ten miles and closing fairly swiftly. There are panic announcements on the radio and TV and the usual tale of exodus. Things are going to be in a mighty sorry mess if you can't do the job in time—"

"I've got to do it in time!" Timothy insisted, glancing up for a moment. "In another hour I should have this rewiring complete. Charter a plane quickly, Mr. Foster—the fastest you can find."

Again Foster vanished, quite willing to take orders at this stage of the proceedings. And Timothy worked on and on, oblivious to everything except his task. When Foster came back he announced that a jet plane was standing by, that it had cost him a small fortune to secure it during the present emergency, when everything that could fly was being commandeered by the Government.

At the end of a further two hours, Timothy looked up at Foster, who was watching anxiously. "Job's finished," he announced. "Let's be on our way."

"And power?" Foster asked. "How do you get that?"

"Simple. Connect to the jet plane's normal generator: it will give me all I need for this model test."

Foster led the way from the room and in a few minutes he and Timothy were being driven at top speed through the sunlit and floodlit streets to the airport. They boarded the jet plane, Timothy keeping his precious apparatus carefully cradled in his arms, and then the journey began.

As the plane screamed its way through starry heavens Timothy gave instructions as to the exact spot he wanted. In any event the pilot could hardly miss it—the only remaining patch at last on a long, clear stretch directly beneath the terrifyingly small gap of blue sky.

"Right!" Timothy exclaimed, and dived for the door.

The moment he descended he saw Henderson hurrying up, and behind him Paget carrying a number of scientific instruments.

"I don't understand why you're here." Timothy said. "I thought you said you were finished with me—"

"I'll explain later. Every moment counts if you're to save that bit of sky. Need any help?"

"Only to connect this instrument to the plane's generator."

In this job no time was lost and the planes normal engine started up. In the screaming din of the engines. Timothy switched on and guided the lens snout of his instrument directly upwards. Everybody looked skywards and no faces had ever been so tense. The seconds passed. Nearby Paget was aiming a small measuring telescope, its object glass traced across with hairlines. After a moment or two he said anxiously, "No change! The gap is still narrowing slowly."

Henderson seemed to have a struggle with himself but he could not help an ironic question: "Sure you have the right instrument and the right plan, Mr. Brown?"

"Absolutely." Timothy was frantically checking the dials of his equipment. "Power normal; wavelength exact; vibration correct for the segregator. The only answer is that I have not enough range. That patch of blue sky is much higher than it appears and I'm not reaching it."

"Then back into the plane we go, and quick," Foster cried.

Hardly anything was said during the take-off, until the mystery of Henderson returned to Timothy's mind.

"Why did you decide to lend a hand?" he asked, puzzled.

"Because," Henderson answered, "I felt it my duty to see if perhaps you really might be able to do something. Mr. Foster made me realize over the phone last night that perhaps I had been too hasty in my judgment and—"

"That story may satisfy Mr. Brown, Dr. Henderson, but it doesn't carry any weight with me," Foster stated flatly. "All you are performing is a face-saving act, knowing perfectly well that if Mr. Brown succeeds this time—and you are reported to have given him no facilities whatever—it would mean the end for you. In other words, I scared you into behaving with some commonsense."

Henderson gave a rather troubled smile. "All right, that's the answer. I have found you—and still find you—a most exasperating person, Mr. Brown."

"Sorry," Timothy apologized humbly, and then wondered why Foster gave him such a glare.

"I knew you'd head for Africa," Henderson added, "so I got there ahead of you."

Timothy sighed. "It doesn't really matter who thinks what any more: the vital thing is to grab that bit of blue sky before it's lost."

The plane climbed to the limits of its height, then began a carefully controlled diagonal descent from the stratospheric heights.

At length, out of the patchwork of black and white below which was sunbathed Earth landscape, there appeared in the searching telescopic instruments what looked like a hole in the dark, below which was an intensely blurred section of Earth itself.

It was the remaining patch of blue sky, but seen from above it was of course not blue—only detectable, as the plane descended lower, as an 'out-of-focus' hole in the surrounding darkness. Timothy Brown was watching it intensely, having made his way into the pilot's cabin. The others crowded behind him through the open door, all normal safety procedures having been abandoned in the urgency of the situation.

"When you're a mile or do above it, fly in a circle around it," Timothy ordered, and the pilot nodded.

"Have you a trapdoor in this plane?" Timothy asked. "To operate this thing of mine I must have a clear space. By that I mean that it won't work through glass that's been treated to block ultra violet: the glass filters the vibration, too."

The pilot shook his head. "Not as such. You can't use the main entrance door because our inside air pressure would blast us outside at this altitude—" He paused as a thought struck him. "What we *do* have, though, are the emergency hatches above the two pilot seats—which can also become ejector seats in a crisis. They open in conjunction with our wanting to eject ourselves from the plane. At this altitude, we'd need to get into a pressure suit, of course."

"Pressure suits?" Timothy asked quickly. "You have some?"

"Two, that's all. One for me and one for the co-pilot." He smiled faintly. "He isn't with us, of course. Foster wouldn't pay for him!"

Timothy's eyes were gleaming. "That will do for me. Now, this is what I have in mind..."

The pilot and the others listened in some astonishment as Timothy outlined his scheme. There were initial protests, especially from Henderson, but at last he gave way.

The cabin was cleared, except for Timothy and the pilot. The door was hermetically sealed. The pilot got into his pressure suit, then helped Timothy to don the other one. After making sure their air supply was working, the pilot de-pressurized the cabin.

Timothy gave instructions through his audiophone on how to link up his apparatus to the power plant with extension cable, gave precise details as to the amount of voltage permitted—which meant the lighting circuit was the best bet as far as power reduction was concerned—then Timothy stood in the co-pilot's seat, his legs secured by straps.

The emergency hatch above him was drawn back, and the pilot manipulated the controls so that the seat rose slowly towards the gap, but stopped short of it by a couple of feet.

Gingerly Timothy stood up, his head and shoulders projecting outside, his projector clutched firmly in his gloved hands.

"Tell me when you're at the right position," Timothy ordered through his suit radio. "I'll do the rest."

"Very well. Mr. Brown."

Timothy was breathing hard at his air apparatus as he surveyed. No god on the Mount of Olympus ever had a better view.

Earth was stretched below, not as a planet but as a vast concave bowl. The normal outlines of landscape were difficult to assess owing to the absence of normal air refraction. The terrain looked lunar in formation, where tall stretches of land caught the sunlight. The remainder was in unrelieved darkness, except for that one spot where things were blurred and infinitely strange.

Above hung the blazing stars and the colossal, prominence-girdled sun. Up here the heat was so furious from those rays both men were perspiring heavily—partly from the nervous tension that gripped them.

"One mile from gap, Mr. Brown," came the pilot's voice in Timothy's earphones.

"Right," Timothy replied promptly. "Keep at that distance and also move to one mile leftwards of the area: that will give me freedom in which to work."

His instructions were obeyed. The plane began to drift slightly, guided by its jets. By degrees it came into the position Timothy wanted. Then he set his instrument down on the roof—secured by magnetic clamps—lowered his head, and sighted the area in the gulf below.

"Keep the plane as steady as you can," Timothy ordered. "Everything depends on it."

"Steady it is, Mr. Brown."

For all that it took several minutes before the pilot achieved a definite balance with the jets. Then Timothy pressed the button on his equipment.

Nothing was visible—no ray or tell-tale glow, but the meters showed that the vibration was definitely being projected at that queer spot in space.

A few minutes elapsed and then Timothy lowered himself back into his seat, leaving the instrument where it was, switched on.

The pilot gave him an enquiring look through his visor.

"Can you lower the seat?" Timothy said. "I'll need to rejoin Henderson and Paget. Only telescopic observation can show us how we're faring."

The pilot opened the cabin door a fraction, and Timothy squeezed quickly though before it was resealed behind him.

Henderson and Paget were anxiously waiting.

"Well?" Paget asked quickly. "Does it work?"

"Can't say just yet," Timothy lifted up his visor. "You've brought your measuring telescope aboard this plane, haven't you?"

Paget nodded and Henderson moved across to it and quickly got it into focus through the window, then he stood aside so that Timothy could make his observations. For nearly five minutes he stood motionless, peering into the lenses. When finally he looked up there was no gleam of triumph in his eye, no sudden ecstasy in his movements. He merely said simply, "Gentlemen, it works!"

"It does!" Henderson cried. "My dear Mr. Brown, how can you ever forgive me for doubting—"

"In the last five minutes," Timothy put in, "there has been no extension of the dark area into the normal area, which means my segregator is an absolute shield between the two. That in turn, means that the Segregator must remain where it is until the last dust atom on this side of the screen has exploded. Only then will it be safe to move it."

"And how long will that be?" asked the pilot anxiously, listening in on the open radio link. "It's by no means easy to keep this plane up here. There are also fuel and myself to be considered. I can't sit here like this indefinitely."

"Half an hour should see the thing finished," Timothy answered. "The reason being that the area is so small— no more than half a mile across. The last atom should have exploded by then. We'd better watch the electronic screen."

Paget switched it on. There was an immediate coruscation of sparks, which revealed that the exploding atoms had not yet finished their activity. There was nothing for it but to wait.

"You're remarkably calm about all this, Mr. Brown," Paget remarked. "Considering the wonderful thing you have done, that is."

"Wonderful?" Timothy looked up from the screen and gave a shrug. "I'd hardly say that. I've simply followed out known scientific laws and seen them operate. Any of you could have done the same."

"We had no basic equations to work on," Henderson grumbled. "And anyhow we don't pretend to have your kink, or streak of genius, whatever it is."

"I notice," Foster said heavily, "that Mr. Brown is no longer in the dog house now he has solved the riddle."

"I can only apologize for my earlier overwrought behaviour," Henderson replied. "You'll accept that. Mr. Brown, and allow mc to tell all the world what you have done?"

"Providing you retract your earlier statements about me, yes." Timothy agreed.

"The explosions have stopped!" Paget exclaimed abruptly.

Immediately there was silence. Everyone studied the screen intently. But it remained blank, except for a quite normal spraying of energy ever and again caused by cosmic radiation.

"It's finished!" Timothy Brown whispered. "The last dust atom has exploded and the chain reaction has come to an end."

It seemed unbelievable for the moment, and Timothy looked as surprised as anybody. He hardly seemed to notice that his hand was being shaken vigorously by each man in turn.

"This must be radioed to the world!" Henderson exclaimed, as genial now as he had been unpleasant before. "Mr. Brown, you are the greatest—"

"Yes, yes, thank you." Timothy interrupted, replacing his pressure suit visor. "If you will forgive me, there are other things I must yet do. I'll keep in touch by radio. Just let me know what reactions you get on that screen."

"Why, what are you going to do beyond recover your instrument?" Foster asked in surprise.

"Make an experiment—and I hope it will prove as much beneficial to you as to me."

Timothy did not explain further. He asked the pilot to open the cabin door so that he could squeeze inside quickly before too much air escaped into the cabin from the inside of the plane.

The men left behind looked at each other anxiously.

"Any idea what he is talking about?" Henderson asked uneasily. "That's one thing about Brown which gets me down: he is always trying something just beyond his knowledge. Why the devil can't he let well alone?"

"I think I know what he's up to," Foster replied. "He said something to me about incorporating the Segregator with the dust destroyer. If that's the case he may start destroying dust again just to prove his point."

"What!" Henderson looked stunned. "He can't! He mustn't! Why didn't we hold him whilst he was in here—?"

"Hello!" came Timothy's voice over the radio. "Are you receiving me?"

"Definitely." Henderson replied. "Now look here, Mr. Brown, you have accomplished a wonderful thing, and it's up to you to let it go at that. Don't start monkeying around with any new experiments: it would be tempting Providence too far."

"I know precisely what I'm doing," Timothy said, with irritating calmness. "It's one thing to have stopped chain reaction, but that in itself is not enough. I want my dust destroyer to become a world beater, and it can if it is made safe, I can only find that out by experiment—and there's no time like the present."

"Don't do it!" Foster implored into the mike. "I'll waive any advantages I might have if you'll—"

"You will perhaps, Mr. Foster, but I can't. I have got to have some way of earning a living, and my dust destroyer is the only chance. I certainly shan't get anything substantial for saving civilization since I ruined everything in the first place. Now tell me if you get a reaction."

Almost immediately there was a spraying of energy across the screen: in fact the old trouble was back in all its devastating fury.

"Oh hell," Henderson groaned. "The idiot's done it!"

"Anything there?" Timothy's voice asked.

"Everything!" Foster yelled. "You damned fool! You've undone the entire work you just did!"

"I know. I've switched off the Segregator and turned the dust-atom vibration on to the part where dust still exists. Now, tell me again."

A pause, and abruptly the screen blanked. No trace of reaction beyond normal cosmic tracks.

"Well?" Timothy asked. "It's stopped, hasn't it?"

"Yes." Henderson told him. "For God's sake, you madman, stop playing tricks with disaster! Come back inside here."

"Coming now. I've found out all I need to know."

And in a few minutes Timothy returned, carrying his instrument in his arms. He set it down and then took off his pressure suit.

"All right," he instructed the pilot over the microphone link. "You need hold the plane no longer. You can re-pressurize the cabin and get out of your suit. You've done a great job! I don't know what Foster's paying you, but I reckon you deserve a handsome bonus—" he broke off and looked at Foster.

Foster looked uneasy, then as Timothy began to frown, he nodded vigorously. "Yes—of course!"

He knew that Timothy's now perfected invention would be netting him a fortune.

"That's settled then!" Timothy resumed. "Best thing now is to return to London. Our job's done and normalcy will slowly come back by natural adjustment."

"You said once how that could happen," Henderson mused, "but I'll be hanged I can recall what you said."

"I said that with the last dust atom exploded it would mean that dust would start to collect again as well as spread from the one tiny area which was never touched. Smoke, drifting spume, all the atmospheric 'refuse' so to speak will gather in no time, and not be annihilated. As it returns so will the clouds, and the general pollution which evidently is essential if we are to go on living."

"The world must be told." Henderson insisted. "And it must be emphasized that you brought salvation about."

Timothy shrugged, but listened just the same as Henderson switched on the long distance radio and gave the news. The reaction of the operator down on Earth was obviously one of profound thankfulness and he promised to transmit a recording of Henderson's message immediately over a worldwide hook-up.

"This means plenty of fun for you when you get back down there," Foster said, nodding to the approaching landscape far below, "And, incidentally, what were you trying out there? Your dust-destroyer again?"

"Just that," Timothy acknowledged. "And this is the point, gentlemen. The instrument embodies a dust destroyer and a Segregator, both operating on different wavelengths, of course, wavelengths indeed that are at opposite ends of the vibratory scale. But about the middle of that scale there is a wavelength that is a combination of both. Do you understand?"

"No," Foster said simply, and Henderson merely shrugged.

"I mean," Timothy elaborated, "that I ran both wavelengths together, linking up the two separate coils, and generated a vibration which destroys dust and at the same time negates chain-reaction."

The men looked at him blankly.

"When I was outside," he continued, "I first destroyed some dust in the only remaining area left in the world, which was when the screen down here sparked once more; then I stopped the small chain reaction effect with the Segregator. After that I took the real chance. I switched both vibrations on at once. According to my mathematics two things could have happened—chain reaction could have restarted and it would have been impossible to stop it in time; or dust would be destroyed without chain reaction.

"Fortunately the latter proved right, as I always thought it would. Therefore 1 have at last created the greatest dust destroyer the world has ever known. And it is perfectly safe."

"And you took a desperate chance like that to prove your—er—mathematics?" Henderson gasped. "Why couldn't you have waited for dust to collect it in the ordinary way, as it certainly will from here on?"

"Because, as I said before. I need money. It may be months before dust settles in the quantity necessary, and in that time I might starve. I want you. Mr. Foster, to have this invention now, so you can pay me advance royalties and get models out to the public. In a word, your fortune is made and so is mine."

"The moment we get home we'll talk business." Foster declared. "And you can take it from me that you'll not lack for money for the rest of your life."

* * * *

Timothy took good care to dodge the crowds at the airport when his plane landed. The radio and TV news had travelled fast and tens of thousands were already converging on London to celebrate. Others wanted to thank Timothy Brown personally, but he was not having any: He still remembered the words of Elsie—that he might be torn to pieces for having caused the trouble in the first place.

He went first to Foster's home and signed the contract for Foster to have exclusive rights in the dust destroyer. Then with a good sized cheque in his pocket, and leaving behind him a highly satisfied businessman, he returned home. By this time it was dark and, as usual, Elsie was lying on the sofa by the gas fire, reading a woman's paper.

"Well, any news?" she asked, struggling up.

"A little." Timothy took off his coat and tossed the cheque nonchalantly into her lap. "That for a start. The other thing is— Haven't you had the TV or radio on?" he asked in astonishment.

"Not tonight. I get sick of bulletins about disease, dark skies and world doom."

"That's a pity, because had you had it on you would have heard how wonderful a man your husband is, how completely he has saved civilization, and how much everybody thinks of him."

"You—you mean—" Elsie slowly unfolded the cheque and stared at it. "Tim! Tim, this is for an absolute fortune!"

"Right." He smiled at her. "And that's only the first instalment. The dust destroyer works at last, even though I've gone rather a long way round to get at it. But never mind!" He caught Elsie round the shoulders as she came towards him. "Everything's going to be all right. The terror is over and the skies will one day become blue again."

He was right—but it was five years before all the world had the sky to which it was accustomed, and even that had to be speeded up by innumerable giant bonfires, chemical fires, the blowing up of volcanoes—in fact everything man could think of in order to create dust and impurities. And, slowly, it began to settle, covering the earth once more with filth and pollution, forming clouds, bringing the rain, just at the time when the last reserves of filtered sea water—for this project had had to be adopted—were running out.

In ten more years the period of the Blackness had become but a memory for which Timothy Brown was at least thankful. He had dropped into wealthy seclusion along with Elsie, and he meant to stay that way.

He rested content in the knowledge that the Kleen-Sweep Dust Annihilator was known from one end of the world to the other, and that it had netted him, and Jacob Foster, a staggering fortune. There was nothing so efficient as Timothy's invention.

"So out of chaos maybe I've given the world something," he remarked to Elsie, as they sat on the terrace one summer evening. "I always knew I was destined for something better than a solicitor's clerk. And, I've got another idea buzzing round."

"Oh?" Elsie looked at him dubiously as he pulled a wad of creased papers from his pocket.

"An idea to make the desert spaces fertile," he explained. "We could alter the climate by changing the wind currents and magnetic lines. There is a difficulty, of course, in that if it went wrong the whole world might either be frozen or scorched into extinction, but I can't see why that should happen—"

"May I see?" Elsie asked quietly, holding out her hand.

"Surely. But I thought you didn't understand science!"

Elsie did not answer. Quite deliberately she took up the lighter from the garden table at Timothy's side. Before he could stop her she had kindled the flame and was watching the charred papers drifting on the breeze.

"No you don't!" she said deliberately.

Timothy sighed and contemplated the soft blue heaven. "Maybe you're right. A little knowledge is a dangerous thing, as somebody once said."

ABOUT THE AUTHOR

British writer **JOHN RUSSELL FEARN** was born near Manchester, England, in 1908. As a child he devoured the science fiction of Wells and Verne, and was a voracious reader of the Boys' Story Papers. He was also fascinated by the cinema, and first broke into print in 1931 with a series of articles in *Film Weekly*.

He then quickly sold his first novel, *The Intelligence Gigantic*, to the American magazine, *Amazing Stories*. Over the next fifteen years, writing under several pseudonyms, Fearn became one of the most prolific contributors to all of the leading US science fiction pulps, including such legendary publications as *Astounding Stories*, *Startling Stories*, *Thrilling Wonder Stories*, and *Weird Tales*.

During the late 1940s he diversified into writing novels for the UK market, and also created his famous superwoman character, The Golden Amazon, for the prestigious Canadian magazine, the Toronto *Star Weekly*. In the early 1950s in the UK, his fifty-two novels as "Vargo Statten" were bestsellers, most notably his novelization of the film, *Creature from the Black Lagoon*.

Apart from science fiction, he had equal success with westerns, romances, and detective fiction, writing an amazing total of 180 novels—most of them in a period of just ten years—before his early death in 1960. His work has been translated into nine languages, and continues to be reprinted and read worldwide.

JOHN RUSSELL FEARN

THE ANJANI SERIES

The Gold of Akada: A Jungle Adventure Novel
Anjani the Mighty: A Lost Race Novel

THE BLACK MARIA SERIES

Black Maria, M.A.: A Classic Crime Novel
The Murdered Schoolgirl: A Classic Crime Novel
One Remained Seated: A Classic Crime Novel
Thy Arm Alone: A Classic Crime Novel
Death in Silhouette: A Classic Crime Novel

THE HERBERT THE DINOSAUR SERIES

A Thing of the Past
The Genial Dinosaur

ADAM QUIRKE SERIES

*The Master Must Die: An Impossible Crime Science Fiction
Novel*
*The Lonely Astronomer: An Impossible Crime Science Fic-
tion Novel*

OTHER BOOKS

1,000-Year Voyage: A Science Fiction Novel
Account Settled: A Science Fiction Mystery
Before Earth Came: Classic Science Fiction Stories
Bury the Hatchet: A Crime Tale
A Case for Brutus Lloyd: A Science Fiction Mystery
The Crimson Rambler: A Crime Novel
Don't Touch Me: A Crime Novel
The Dust Destroyer
Dynasty of the Small: Classic Science Fiction Stories
The Empty Coffins: A Mystery of Horror

The Fourth Door: A Mystery Novel
From Afar: A Science Fiction Mystery
Fugitive of Time: A Classic Science Fiction Novel
The G-Bomb: A Science Fiction Novel
Here and Now: A Science Fiction Novel
Into the Unknown: A Science Fiction Tale
Last Conflict: Classic Science Fiction Stories
Legacy from Sirius: A Classic Science Fiction Novel
The Man from Hell: Classic Science Fiction Stories
The Man Who Was Not: A Crime Novel
Manton's World: A Classic Science Fiction Novel
Moon Magic: A Novel of Romance (as Elizabeth Rutland)
One Way Out: A Crime Novel (with Philip Harbottle)
Pattern of Murder: A Classic Crime Novel
Reflected Glory: A Dr. Castle Classic Crime Novel
Robbery Without Violence: Two Science Fiction Crime Stories
Rule of the Brains: Classic Science Fiction Stories
Shattering Glass: A Crime Novel
The Silvered Cage: A Scientific Murder Mystery
Slaves of Ijax: A Science Fiction Novel
Something from Mercury: Classic Science Fiction Stories
The Space Warp: A Science Fiction Novel
The Time Trap: A Science Fiction Novel
Valley of Pretenders: Classic Science Fiction Stories
Vision Sinister: A Scientific Detective Thriller
Voice of the Conqueror: A Classic Science Fiction Novel
What Happened to Hammond? A Scientific Mystery
Within That Room!: A Classic Crime Novel
World Without Chance: Classic Science Fiction Stories

www.ingramcontent.com/pod-product-compliance
Lightning Source LLC
Chambersburg PA
CBHW020146180626
46810CB00004B/1754